RALEIGH REVIEW
LITERARY & ARTS MAGAZINE

VOL. 14.1
SPRING 2024

RALEIGH REVIEW

VOL. 14.1 SPRING 2024

PUBLISHER
Rob Greene

EDITOR-IN-CHIEF
Landon Houle

FICTION EDITOR
Jessica Pitchford

POETRY EDITOR
Leah Poole Osowski

EDITORIAL STAFF / FICTION
Dailihana Alfonseca, Chas Carey,
Madison Cyr, Susan Finch, Robert
McCready, Jeff McLaughlin, Erin
Osborne, Allison Frase Reavis,
Shel Senai

BOARD OF DIRECTORS
Joseph Millar, Chairman
Dorianne Laux, Vice Chair
Landon Houle, Member
Bryce Emley, Member
Will Badger, Member
Tyree Daye, Member
Rob Greene, Member

ASSISTANT FICTION EDITOR
Erin Osborne

SENIOR COPYEDITOR
Elaina Ellis

COPYEDITOR
Charlene Pierce

EDITORIAL STAFF / POETRY
Chelsea Harlan, D. Eric Parkison,
Sam Piccone, Melanie Tafejian,
Annie Woodford

ILLUSTRATOR
Nora Beers Kelly

LAYOUT & PAGE DESIGN
Alexis Olson

LITERARY PUBLISHING PROGRAM
Alaina Haywood Jones
WCPSS-SAU Early College Intern

Raleigh Review, Vol. 14, No. 1, Spring 2024
Copyright © 2024 by *Raleigh Review*

Raleigh Review founded as *RIG Poetry*
February 21, 2010 | Robert Ian Greene

Cover image "Fragments" by Christen Noel Kauffman
Cover design by Alexis Olson

ISBN: 978-1-59498-198-2

Raleigh Review is printed and bound via Fernwood Press in Oregon, U.S.A., and
distributed globally via Ingram.

Raleigh Review, PO Box 6725, Raleigh, NC 27628
Visit: raleighreview.org

RALEIGH REVIEW

table of contents

poetry cont. —————————————————————

contributors —————————————————————

RALEIGH REVIEW

VOL. 14.1 SPRING 2024

FROM THE EDITOR

THIS IS OUR SPRING ISSUE, but because of the nature of our production calendar, it's January as I'm writing this note. It's a cold day by our expectations here in South Carolina—forty-nine degrees now and a predicted twenty-seven by the coldest part of the night. I'm sitting in our drafty living room with a glowing space heater pulled dangerously close to my legs, and through the windows, the last of the day is dimming, the shadows growing dark.

Another day is done, but we're still new to resolutions. Yesterday, I read a list on the internet that said if you want to be healthier, you should do these four things: be grateful, spend time with your pets, stand up every hour, and floss. I rolled my eyes when I read it—the rolling nearly a reflex, some kind of teenage residue—but you know I had to click a few times to read the whole list, so eye-rolling aside, I'm aware I'm betraying my own guilty interest in this likely sponsored content. And because we're friends, I'll tell you that despite my attempts at a tough attitude, the list keeps popping up in my thoughts even if I usually can only remember three of the four tenets.

I think I've come to that point in life when my memory is about 75% functional, and I've given up on making my own resolutions. I just do what the internet tells me to do. For my own part, I've moved from resolutions to general efforts. I *generally* try to eat healthy things. I generally try to exercise. I generally try to read more.

That last one, the reading bit, is probably the one for which I feel the most resolve. I've bought what amounts to a stack of new books over the last couple of weeks. This is also the time of year I think about subscriptions, and I guess I'm not alone.

"I miss the newspaper," my mom said during our recent holiday visit.

"You could subscribe," I said.

"Yeah," Mom said. "But I can't tell what's online and what's actually paper."

I nod because I know she doesn't really want me to pull up the site and help her navigate the system. I know she just wants to bemoan, to blow off a little steam about the complications of modern life. She doesn't want to figure it out as much as she wants things to be like they were—when reading a newspaper meant smudgy fingertips and passing sections back and forth across a table.

I use the good three-quarters of my memory to think back to those Sunday afternoons. Sometimes we would have been to church, and sometimes we wouldn't have, but the noon hunger was always sharper and somehow always better satiated after you'd listened to a speech about sinning and being forgiven. Once the last hymn had been sung and the final announcements made, we'd practically run to the car. We'd make a quick stop at the Thrift Mart and pick up some lunch meat and the *Dallas Morning News*. We'd race home, throw off our itchy dresses and throw on our worn-thin t-shirts and stretch shorts. A ham and cheese sandwich with a dill pickle never tasted better than it did sitting on a splayed *Parade* insert. In those moments, scandalized by celebrity gossip and inspired by upcoming exhibits at the art museums in the city, Monday was still a lifetime away.

I've been thinking a lot about those Sunday afternoons. After we returned home from the holidays, I went so far as to look up subscription options to the *Dallas Morning News*, which I texted to Mom. (She still thinks the easier option will be to pick up a copy at the grocery store.) I'm a long way from Dallas now, so it'd make more sense to get a newspaper out of Columbia, the largest city near me. But after some clicking and scrolling, I was saddened to discover *The State* doesn't deliver to our rural area. So I'm subscribing to our local newspaper and some other magazines too.

Like I said, you won't be reading this note until we're a few months into 2024, but maybe for a minute, you can re-imagine that new year state of mind. Maybe you, too, want to read more or encourage others to. In all your browsing of books, newspapers, and magazines, I hope you'll consider renewing your subscription to *Raleigh Review* or perhaps giving a subscription as a gift to someone else.

You're holding an issue in your hands now, so you probably already know that we feature thoughtful, engaging, and entertaining literature and art, and I'm betting there's someone in your life who would like to see that kind of work, too. This time around, in addition to our sections of poetry, art, and long-form fiction, we're thrilled and honored to present the winner of our Flash Fiction Prize, Doug Crandell's "Cyclone Seeder." We're also proud to feature the work of our finalists, Cyn Nooney, Anna Schachner, and Philip Schaefer. Congratulations to all, and a thanks to our fiction team for their careful selections.

I'll do you a favor and spare you the churchy reprimands, but I hope you enjoy this issue as much as a Sunday newspaper. I hope you crack the spine under your elbow while you eat something you love as much as I love pickles. I hope every now and then, you read a line aloud, even if only the cat is listening. Thank the writers and the artists for their work. Heck, give them a standing ovation. And when you're done, even if you don't want to, take a minute to floss.

There you are, healthier and happier already.

Happy 2024, everyone! ◆

Landon Houle, editor-in-chief

PHILIP SCHAEFER

CARNIVOROUS GREEN

This morning's internet paper reads that the new generation craves itself
more than intimacy. The image of the image of. To be heard but not

held. To wither alone knowing not what you want, but who you don't.
This the time of year when I walk the dog & watch as the earth burns

its own face. I wait for the sundews to bloom, the snapdragons
to breathe their holy fire. I text a photo of a lilac wall to my mother

so she knows I'm alive, so she can feel my voice inside her mind.
She is aging in the smaller parts of her body. A flytrap wilting

toward Venus, a moonflower lighting its silken body into whatever
stiff bed comes next. Some days I slip into an afternoon dive

just to hear ice break down in a tumbler. For the chatter of birds
the men in this town have become. I wouldn't trade anything

to be this loud, this quiet, in tempo. We all need to know a hurt
that cannot be named. It starts beneath the skin, then buds, then sings.

AMY RATTO PARKS

FORECASTING

Under the blood moon, the mown

lawns will hold low and flat as turf.

The cars will sit along the curbs

and the cats will peer out, shadow-huddled

in wait. I stand at the glass of my door

checking the light on the mountain.

They say the moon will turn red

and they say that an eclipse is coming.

All I see are leftover balloons from a party

broken loose and blowing through yards,

gold and green—their thin skins,

their empty selves—just this close to breaking.

DOUG CRANDELL

CYCLONE SEEDER

MY MOTHER is milky white in Urbana, Indiana, the color of 2% and Wonder Bread, yet she applies orange tint to look as though she still toils outdoors under the sun's rays. But she has left the fields for the factory because it doesn't bend to rain, hail, tornadoes, or early frosts. Inside the Cyclone Seeder factory, it's always warm and clear, but just as dangerous as picking corn. Her worries aren't losing an arm in an auger. She frets about the men, the ugly hunger in their eyes. Not all of them, of course, but enough to make her think of the word "pack" at break time, a chilling, sickening word when brought to bear on humans.

She works in a small factory where men rule. At night, she returns home so our father can start his shift in another factory where acoustic tiles are made, drop-down ceilings and foiled-backed insulations are shipped across the Hoosier tundra, up north in slag train cars, across the frozen border and into Canada. In our drafty rented house, they have ten minutes to chat as their shifts change, a crease on my father's brow and a deeper sadness in his brown beagle eyes. His tenderness is a prelude, her intentional upbeat energy a whole other type of augur. He gives her dandelions, and she hands him a hot thermos. Even after he has left in the battered pickup, our mother watches out the long ecclesiastical windows, the only nice thing about the dilapidated house, watches him as if he were heading to the moon.

Factories of their own, they belong to two different unions. They have failed at farming, have lost it all on the land, and now they join all the small manufacturers in places like Kokomo, Peru, Shipshewana, Trafalgar, and Mudsock. Everyone knows what our mother's hands assemble because all you have to say is Cyclone without adding the seeder part. Sometimes on the rare occasion when someone doesn't know, she mimes it, as if playing charades, cranking an invisible handle, pretend seeds flying from the wheel, landing on loam to sprout. She says she likes that she makes things that sow, that create the reaping, the last word sounding like weeping because of her Vigo County coal mine accent.

ONE NIGHT, under an amber summer brimming with floating fireflies, she does not come back to the house. Our father smokes Salems from one lit end to another, tapping his work boot and looking at his silver, cheap wristwatch. By seven p.m., a man accustomed to shifts, to being on time and ready to work, he calls the Cyclone Seeder office. He imagines she's taken overtime or can't start the rusty Malibu, but his cheeks are ruddy, and we've only seen them like that when he's sick, running a fever, fighting a migraine after a sixteen-hour shift.

He nods, standing with the phone receiver to his red ear, taps the cigarette into the cuff of his pants and carefully places the phone back in its worn yellow cradle, gently like we've seen him do when he holds a baby, self-conscious of his strong hands. He swallows. One of us asks where she is, and he turns and looks out the long, bleary windows. He tells us to get ready for bed and then phones Mrs. Kiefaber, the sitter, who doesn't answer.

During the night, while we sleep, he stands like a collie at the front door, striding onto the porch and back again. The smell of smoke and burnt coffee and sulfur matches wafts up to us. One of us has been sneaking to the banister to spy, report back. We are under threadbare quilts, saliva-stained but clean pillowcases against our restless cheeks, the smell of her bleach like her perfume.

In our reluctant sleep, fitful, one of us sweating through the night, the others dry-mouthed and sobbing, no dreams arrive, just darkness and dread. In the bleak dawn, there is no lag, no separation, no distance between what our father feared the most, to what is most present. We will not know until two decades later how her body was found, in a fescue ditch, along the roadway that led to the Cyclone Seeder factory. She is pale and bruised, neck twisted. The waning moon bounces off her soft body and back up to the stars, to the nebula, to a calloused hand. In the paper, it says a union brother killed her, and one of us is now afraid of her brothers.

THE DAYS BEFORE she's in the ground, we eat food that is not hers, scalloped potatoes, chipped beef, and baked macaroni the color of a sun setting. One of us won't go to the casket, won't line up and accept the dire conclusion. That one's throat burns with hate, with loss, with the taste of oil and sawdust and work sweat when what he wants is the taste of her JC Penney lipstick, of her cheek powder smelling like brown sugar, her soft hair ripe with balsam.

In the funeral home, there is a commotion, and adults arrive like dazed wasps from alcoves and side rooms. They all try to chaperone, to guide and show the way. Once one of us kicks at a floral display and it topples, the rest of the blooms and wired structures with plastic gold leaf seem to collapse in on themselves, and our father tries to catch them all but cannot, and he's left with righting the ones that remain, straightening them so those mourning will see he can put his work to the task and make it until the end of his cursed shift, his rough hands trembling against the awful air of the funeral home, under its flickering cruel lights. One of us runs to him and he kneels, and then all are sobbing into his Kmart suit jacket. He sobs too, and then it is quiet as people recede, the coffin's surface reflecting light that all of us hate. ◆

CYN NOONEY
EIGHT-ZIP

FOR HER EIGHTIETH BIRTHDAY we traveled to see Mother in her tiny house on the Sound. The blowout party we'd been planning for months had to be scrapped. The surprise tickets we'd purchased for Mother to finally see the Rolling Stones in concert were relisted on StubHub. What about us, our husbands said, we can still use them. Yeah, echoed our kids, it's the main reason we were willing to come. As if she wanted to get sick, we said. We're in this together. We're all disappointed.

Over the telephone, Mother warned us that she had a cannula up her nose, an oxygen tank by her side. Plus, the house paint was peeling, her shrubbery overgrown. No matter, we said, we've all seen much worse.

The nurse said to take turns visiting, so we drew up a schedule and then straws. Who would go first?

We all hoped for last.

But I'm not helpless, Mother insisted. Or contagious. She pleaded with us to let her host a group meal. I don't ask for much, she said. Which was partially true. Is it wrong to want all my loves in one place, she went on. No one had the strength to say no. We texted each other from our separate VRBOs and said let's do whatever she wishes. At least this once. We won't stay too long or get too close.

We were four freckled sisters. Our father had longed for a boy.

The catered spareribs were dry, the coleslaw too sweet. The ears of corn weighed down our plates made of paper. Many dropped to the floor. Sweeping we were good at. That we could do. We checked Mother's pulse meter. Adjusted her oxygen. Upward. Doled out her pills and water, a squirt of banana pudding. Her appetite was small. Mother told us the doctor said she would no longer be able to go ice skating or skiing. Too hard on her lungs. We tried not to laugh. We tried not to say, well, yeah, why are you acting surprised? Or forlorn. When was the last time you went?

Still, we knew that day would come for us too.

Plastic tubing circled Mother's lap, which she released through her fingers as the children pushed her around on a small-wheeled seat. I'm everyone's pet, she said, I've got my own leash. They skidded her toward the sliding glass door. Careful, we shouted. Don't tip her over! Or unplug the machine! Mother said, Oh, hush. I want a family photo on the deck. Are you sure, we asked. Really? Everyone's here, she said, and it's been forever. Quit making a stink.

Our eyes met above the kitchen counter strewn with clumps of baked beans, empty-bottled IPAs, and her boxcar of meds. Was she right? How long had it been? We won't show her the pictures, we silently agreed. She'll hate how she looks, how ghoulish and stooped. She'll hate how lightly our hands touch her shoulders as though she might break. She'll see right through our Saran smiles and splayed feet.

Watch out, or I'll ram your shins, she cried.

Out on the deck, slashes of tangerine streaked the lavender sky. Beneath us, the water churned its hello. I'll always remember this, I'm imprinting it on my heart, said Mother as we attempted selfies. She was seated in the middle, lipstick staining her teeth. She looked like our grandmother right before Nana died. Perhaps we were more scared than she.

I'll be super pissed-off if you don't show me the pictures, Mother said afterward. Super pissed-off was how we'd been raised. Reluctantly, we tapped our screens to enlarge the photos and passed around our phones. Her delight was the size of a shore at low tide. Look at us, she said. Oh, my. There's been no better day.

So true, we lied. But now it's late, and we must go.

No. Please. I don't want you to.

We'll be back in the morning. First thing. You need your rest.

How dare you turn this on me, said Mother, and with surprising vigor she scooped up the shoes that we'd left near the door, hawking them one at a time toward our heads. Cut and run, huh? After devoting my whole life to you?

Our children laughed. They scurried to fetch more of our flip-flops and sneakers. Here, Gran, they said, keep throwing. Hard as you can.

We covered our faces. Rubber soles hit our ears and our necks.

I hope it stings, said Mother. I hope you feel every last ache.

She chucked another shoe. The count was up to eight.

Enough, we said, and pressed down our mother's hands. Scram, we told our kids and our spouses. We've got this, we said, even though we had nothing at all.

We lowered our sprawling rumps down to the floor near Mother's soft-slippered feet and turned our faces upward like courteous kinder-gartners on the first day of school. She chewed on a hangnail, biting till it bled. Her mouth moved like Jagger's. Then she punched the air with her fist. One blast, and that's it, she spurted. Time is a thief in the night no one can catch.

Her head fell forward. A string of drool swung from her lip.

After a moment, we gently removed her slippers then rubbed her tough, thirsty soles and her thick, starchy ankles, tracing the veins that long ago brought us breath. As children we'd handed over our hearts, so trusting and whole, and she'd carried these wet, pulpy organs around and around, wherever she went, aiming to be tender even if sometimes she tripped. We shifted closer to her, tightening our circle. Go on, we said. Get it all out. Otherwise? Brace yourself, for these will be coming your way. We held up her slippers, uncertain if she was pretending. Could she still see us?

We waited for whatever was left. ◆

CYN NOONEY

MAYBE EVERYTHING

WHEN OUR SON came home, the tree was up, the presents wrapped with bright ribbon. Let's get a good look at you, we said. We were candy cane happy. Gummy and sweet. The cat hid beneath the hutch. I thought you liked dogs, he said. We put on Santa hats and matching pajama bottoms, drank spiked hot cocoa in mugs.

He was trying, we could tell.

Our drapes were open. Strands of lights glimmered in the neighborhood. Wreaths hung on doors. It's so quiet here, our son said, has it always been this quiet, and we said we weren't sure. Or couldn't remember. For dinner we served mashed potatoes with gravy and steak, his favorite. Do you like your classes, we asked, your roommates? Do you like your jobs, he said, each other? Just kidding, he laughed, and we could see that he took good care of his teeth.

I get by, he said. Don't worry about me. Tell us how not to, we said. That's on you, our son replied, and took his plate over to the sink.

He went upstairs and showered then came back down and stretched out on the floor. He stuck his arm beneath the cabinet. Here kitty, kitty. Seconds later, he said, What the fuck, what kind of monster is this? My hand.

It was scratched and bleeding. We found Band-Aids and an old tube of Neosporin. May we put it on for you, we wanted to ask. Like when you were little. We wanted to hold him close. We wanted to kiss his man-boy neck. We wanted to take his hands between ours and look both ways before crossing the street. We wanted to say one two three ready and swing him high, wee wee wee.

I'm okay, he said. I've got this. But we weren't convinced. We wanted to brush the hair from his eyes. We want to see you, we almost said. But we knew better than to push.

Our son left to see friends. We went to bed. Our pajamas were wrinkled, our tongues dense with whiskey. It eked out in bubbles and burps, and we turned our faces toward the wall. Like all those other times we couldn't sleep. We waited to hear the key in the lock. It was three, and then it was four. He didn't answer our texts. Or pick up our calls. What if we phone the police, we wondered. But then, no, he might never come back. Trust is critical. Everyone knows that.

We thought, let's text his friends. We still had their numbers. We tried to figure out what to say and who should send the message, but after reaching no consensus, we got in the car. Some of the houses were still lit up in twinkling lights, which provided a stab of comfort. Our eyeglasses turned steamy. With our bad breath we blew on our fingers. Then crossed them. Tight, so tight. We circled the neighborhood again and again before driving to the park where kids in high school went to smoke weed and have sex. High school, we scoffed—try middle school.

We'll find him, we told ourselves. We will. Everything will be all right. He had on a corduroy jacket? Those beat-up boots? He's tall, we said, too tall to hide.

We would do it all over again, we said. Every last thing. Well, maybe not some things.

He'll come back, we said. We told this to each other over and over. We did our best. Right? We gave him everything.

Oh, we said, maybe—

Then we turned on the other. It was something we were good at. We pulled over. Bared our canines. One of us got out of the car and called our son's name again and again with growing alarm. What would he say if he saw us—For the love of Christ, get your own lives? The other one revved the engine and shouted, Get back in the car. This will get us nowhere!

Nowhere we'd been. Nowhere we knew. Holding each other back was nothing we practiced. Our voices rose higher and higher then dipped and dimmed, swallowed by the night along with our son who had never been ours to keep. ◆

ASHLEY SEITZ KRAMER

TO PASS AROUND A PROMISE

My uncle felled the eighty-foot spruce
& my mother counted fifty rings as thin
as the distance between rearview years.
The object of feeling lags behind the feeling.
Every day for ten days I walked a mile
to the bridge to see the blue heron stalking
fish in the muddy river. *We arrive at some things*
because they make us happy. The river wouldn't clear
but the heron & I began to expect each other.
I watched the heron watch me until day eleven
then I left. *Think of the promise as a situation.*
I wake up away from you, uncertain: images
of crashing into matchstick trees nightmare
my sleep. Sometimes my dreams catch fire,
sometimes the mountains do. Nothing
to worry about, you insist, but I know exactly
what you can & cannot promise, what chaos
in this world cannot be ordered: even my grand-
father, who believed in a powerful god, knew
the shuffled deck of cards softens to cloth.
'I promise you' slides into 'the promise of'—
what, safety? My love, we both know better.
You are a heron hopping rocks. *The very*
expectation of happiness gives us a specific image
of the future. Who am I there?
How black is my dress?

The italicized text in this poem is from Sara Ahmed's *The Promise of*
Happiness (2010).

14

SEVEN ATTEMPTS AT QUANTUM INTIMACY

1

to think that anyone
could know anyone else
that anyone knows herself
to know you I
find that moving away
is useful like a portrait painter
gathering perspective
and maybe more supplies
I like blurring at the edges I like
the details crisp and centered
where else would
your beautiful nose go?
city lights wink to me below
a river of lures for common fish
that swim and dream and wish wish
wish to be caught

2

my body disappoints me
as if we are separate as if
we agreed to something else
not this erosion it's true I've had
few reasons to contemplate
the tailbone but I understand

such mistakes now: to take

for granted the absence of pain

to sit (a gift) I want

your mouth close enough

to whisper *I'm sorry*

that hurts my jaw

aches into the past

3

so many windows

in this new house

the birds our birds!

they clatter they collapse

smear of feather faint

as dawn memory

of a memory of flight

how to catalog our losses?

with what thickness

of graphite should I take

notes? Brent says

not to worry about a

black widow bite but

listen: the water filter

is humming our song

through rust

4

virga is a word I just learned

to describe something I've seen

many times before *virga*
expands into other
places of meaning I must
feel an emotion
before I recognize its arrival
suspension before touchdown
though sometimes nothing
ever touches
down I am interested
in my own weather in yours
what doesn't touch down
the weather woman floats
across our television a dress
the color of clouds and I do not
think she is qualified
to promise anything

5

matter can be transformed
but not eliminated matter
can change but not go away
are feelings like this?
in evening I am a raw
potato of sadness in morning
yellow apple of optimism
here is a beautiful acorn
a perfect acorn and another
one more we'll throw them
in the front yard you said

and see what grows

6

I ask what burns
and you instruct while
we forage like the first
partners searching
as we are into evening
it is difficult
and possible to steady
in a canyon we bend
and straighten
our thin bundles build
you are almost frenzied
this and *this* and *this*
you chant
burn easy

7

I never used to kill spiders
but tonight I drowned
one the color of clear corn
in the toilet then felt
eight times smaller
than my actual mass
and more guilty for being
alive in such a casual way
what am I doing
with all this time?

spiders have ten legs

but they use two as hands

spinnerets of sorrow!

spinnerets of joy!

I had no right to drown

that spider all I do is

send emails about emails

despair covers me

like a clean warm sheet

it is so hard not to harm

LEMON, LICHEN

" ... the past tense turns a sentence dark ..."
Larry Levis, "Childhood Ideogram"

The moment I name a thing
I sense a fluctuating accuracy—
the grocery bag with one fewer lemon
than I purchased, so hard to tell,
but yes, it's lighter, a lemon's worth.
The moment I begin to name a thing,
the moment it is named, it darkens
in its own space of nameness: bright
green pepper browning on the vine
toward red, or something soiled.
Please understand: I'm a lover
of the dark. I don't fear it now
as many do. My eyes adjust.
I see what moves. I still see you.
The light, it never leaves, the light
has never left. Last week in Ohio
my mother bent down low to stroke
the lichen growing under one
old tree. Lichen, from the Greek
for lick, what eats around itself.
My mother is so proud
of how it covers.

PAUL FREIDINGER

WORKING

I was cutting river willows
that had fallen into the lagoon
water black from tannic acid,
balancing on a log, gripping
a limb with one hand,
leaning like a gymnast
with the other, working
the saw as if I were punching
a drunk down to the mat,
Carolina sun searing
and making me sick.

This is a fact, not alleged,
and I kept at it, sweat
burning my eyes, I blinked,
lowered my nose to the surface,
this was no mirror;
no, hundreds of minnows
like flecks of coal were laboring,
too, blindly treading
the murk above the mud,
the way we all came out of it once
in some primordial, four-act play.
We swam, surfaced, breathed,
invented a language.

Distracted by the world
beneath me and the one behind me,
forgot how I got here
on a tenuous branch, clearing
brush away so I could see

while the other dimension
was there all along, working
to remind me how.

ANNA SCHACHNER

THE BEE'S (STICKY, CERTAIN) KNEES

THE TRAILER MARQUEE outside the country church read "Blessing of the Animals Today," so we—tired and angry and loveless, reduced to skin and bone— pulled over and took ourselves inside. Because it was a Tuesday, we were probably too late and expected to find only some dog hair left on the carpet down the middle aisle, a few overlooked rabbit pellets on the pews, a rogue lizard hiding in the lectern since Sunday, nibbling pages of the hymnbook for sustenance. How long it took God's favor to dissipate once it was given, we didn't know.

Yet the little church was full of sunlight and creatures. The smell of basil and thyme, like our kitchen on the nights we used to cook together, floated in the air, so thick we could almost cup it in our hands. Jesus, or at least a robed young man in sneakers, palms pressed together, stood on

the altar, calling out names. We offered each other a solemn glance and nodded. We sat in the back pew under stained glass, turned away from each other, listening, though we had failed at that for years. In the pew in front of us, a girl with a braid down her back lifted a jar and pressed her lips against the glass.

> *Sir Bubba, the pug*
> *Three Spots, the adolescent cow*
> *Mildred, the chicken*
> *Goldie Hawn, the fish*
> *Goopy, the baby goat*

With each name, there was scuffling and "excuse me"s and toenails against tiles and some grunting and panting—did we dare to remember grunting and panting?—before a semi-circle slowly formed in front of the altar. All the animals were draped in garlands of flowers, and with their silence, they *honored* the petals, leaves, and stems, all the way back to the seeds; even Goldie Hawn swam the circumference of a fishbowl wrapped with a strand of yellow daisies. Then the people—Mildred the chicken alone had four accompanying her—began to sing, speaking for all the animals, as a fiddle player in the front pew began his praise. The pastor smiled and dipped a small bouquet of herbs into a bowl to sprinkle water on Mildred, Goopy, and Sir Bubba, who now sat atop Three Spots.

The girl with the jar turned to study the door, then settled her gaze on us. We glanced at each other as if to ask, *Does she see that we don't belong among such pageantry?* We had our own. After all, marriage undone is its own parade of pain. And where was God's protection in the last-chance-for-romance hotel getaway we had just left?

The pastor called them forward:

> *Cheeky, the Squirrel*
> *Luna, the cat*
> *Rambo, the turtle*
> *Hansel and Gretel, the German shepherds*
> *Pretty Please, the parrot*

There were so many favors, so many flowers, so many hands reaching for fur or feathers. All of God's creation.

"Where is your pet?" the little girl asked us, her chin propped on the top edge of the pew. We smiled and shook our heads, but she held up her jar. A very still bee lay at the bottom, its back legs folded underneath its body and its wings spread nearly wide. "We think Bebe's legs are broken."

We leaned in to listen. We had been waiting for the broken to be called.

The girl pressed together her lips before she blew a small puff of air through one of the holes in the lid. "Too much nectar," she said, sadly. "That's what happens when bees get nectar from flowers—it sticks to their legs, their knees mostly." She squinted through the glass. "Tiny little bees," she said, nodding hopefully. "Mama says they put the 'be' in 'believe.'"

She turned back around, and we waited—oh, how we waited!—for Bebe to be carried to the altar so that we could follow, so that we could ask and ask and ask for God's favor, conspicuous at last. ◆

PHILIP SCHAEFER
TUGBOATS

I'VE BEEN CHEATING on you my whole life, I think out loud to the bath-room mirror. I'm talking to her, some other me, my child, anyone who might listen. I move my eyebrows up and down, stick out my tongue. I want to be more punk rock, to care less. Dotty's on the toilet behind me singing poorly *a doo run run run a doo run run*, hair over her face like one of those doodle furballs. I tell her to flush, knowing I'll never be that happy today.

She wants me to make her an over-medium bullseye, so I cut out a circle in the rye and hold it up to my eye, go bloodshot to freak her out, entertain myself. Natalie tells me to stop playing with her food. We're going to the carnival this afternoon, so at least I have $14 funnel cakes to look forward to. Missoula's perfect this time of year. The sun explodes its confetti in every shade of cotton candy. The mountains hold themselves upright as if with something to prove. It's like the town, the weather, the air, are all rehearsing for something. A royal funeral, a stray at the pound.

We buckle into the Tilt-A-Whirl and hold hands, the three of us flayed flat together like biblical sacrifices. I close my eyes as daylight fills my lungs and squeeze tight the little digits crawling in my palm. Even though I can't get her stupid song out of my head, I'm grateful. She's alive. We're alive. I have a child, a forever asset.

Once we collect ourselves and the nausea starts to dissipate, we drift like jellyfish toward the food stands. Dotty wants three funnel cakes. I want some hot dog with my mustard. Natalie wants to rest her legs. Her knee still bothers her occasionally, even after all these years, an acute reminder of my failures, my ghosts. I throw the little one onto my shoulders while Natalie finds a picnic table. We return with $44 of unrecognizable glory, a scene from a Peter Pan movie, the Robin Williams one.

Dusk is starting to fall, and the sky begins its operatic crescendo. Dotty's getting tired, so we wander car-bound, Natalie and I shoulder bumping along the way like tugboats at war. The dishes in the kitchen, that endless rock of Sisyphus, whisper my name, as do the three beers in the fridge. I crack a Mexican lager and put on yellow latex gloves. After putting the kiddo down, Natalie walks up behind me and wraps her arms into parentheses around my waist as a thank you, an I see you. We haven't made love in weeks, but the intention is there. I scrub the Dutch oven as if scratching off a lottery ticket. I want to see my reflection in the pond. I want it so clean it whistles out a million bucks.

Natalie gets ready for bed, so I turn on the tube. God, who even says that anymore, but I kind of like it. I scroll with the boredom, that existential late-night itch where all productivity ceases, where humanity cocoons itself into its own void, willfully, wantonly, animals magnetized to their predators. I land on *Planet Earth* and wake up at 4:30, dead to the couch, the world, this foreign house and its mountain sounds. I get up and fall into the bed, Natalie shifting over to her corner with the sheets, that endless argument of sleep.

I fade into a half dream. We're on a roof over the ocean. We're not flying, but there's no suspension holding us either. The sky is a dalmatian of hot white with several black clouds polka-dotting the periphery. An

owl lands on my shoulder, and fear shoots through the veins in my legs. It's talking to me. It says you can do better than this. It hooks into my flesh. Daddy, my tummy hurts. And I freefall back into mortality, the ocean of fatherhood, this Dramamine existence. ◆

MATTHEW MINICUCCI

NOSTALGIA

The porch birdfeeder plays an important role in *something something oh fuck it*. I don't have to explain how red the paint might have been, once, or what my mom's hair looked like in winter. The weak-nuclear force in the boson-voice of my father. I'll just stay here for a spell. Pointed, these swords crossed and uncrossed. How provincial. Finally, the friars are out. Zoom link won't work and could you send again, please? And could you send again, please? Please let me be in the long slip of afternoon, the ocean's just empty room. What loss in language? You say *gap* or *void* and I say *lacus,* Latin for *pond* or *lake.* Water loves a hollow, of course. A word made true only in its impossible sound. Is there such a thing as a word sprung from nothing but the wallow of empty stung? I've placed brackets in the moody cloud of this day. And this one too. I've pointed to the pilcrows resting right off the impromptu laundry rope line. *The thing about most space is it's never filled,* you said. Don't be that way. It's true: there's a fire in Alexandria I forgot to tell you about; the cream just-stirred into the coffee. Once, my Greek Drama professor was chased by a man through the wine-dark streets of Thessaloniki after finding a play. What's lost is lost. What looks up looks up at him like a solitary serpent's tooth.

NOSTALGIA

One body is always lesser than the other. Simple. One is light and one is lighter still. One leaves one and then boats or bills of birds you've never heard all spill their songs like *pintar* the Spanish paint or Pindar the Greek poet. In victory, *what is anyone?* What is any one not? But you don't know the one named for the bright red nose. There's never heard and never more and nevermind the tool left like a dagger for you-know-what. I do. That's the problem. I cleaned the bathroom today because my friend is dying of you-know-what. That's what his wife told me over the phone: he's dying. Mucus on the mother-fucking rug. Moratorium on sleeping together. Like all these lost tongues: how unsatisfying. How sub-orbital in its frame, its new moon, its satellite of a satellite and that's how I feel most mornings: periapsis of a memory of a memory of a memory. Portishead on the radio. All so petrified to move, we are. She said [blank] and the world lurched on same as it always does: fast. Imperceptibly so. Neck-snapped. Bat above the eyelash-ed scar. Quicker still. Then slower. Do it again, but slower. What if I placed my hand here right above the knee? Above the clavicle? *Cenote. See note bene.* What then? What's left after this red moon light goes dark then blink, then blink, then blind, then gone.

ERIN JONES BENNETT

ALLELOPATHY

In the morning we say nothing.
There's an apple left whole

on the counter. Nothing
can come of this.

Last night the moon
let out its breath, vibrant

across the living room floor
and our ankles.

Windows open, I remember
the night-noise was edible.

So what is it with sunlight,
your eyes looking anywhere else

but these two bodies, like there's an exit
for tenderness. The truth is

there are ways to make you stay
past summer. Surely, late August

will assume you, thin and bitten
down to only rind.

ELEGY

Just last summer we took
the rods to Rodanthe Pier,
trying for Red and Black Drum.
Back and forth we went
all morning—jigs, cut bait,
anything to snag a kiss
on the line. I remember
the boy who caught you
with his rogue cast,
a circle hook snagging
the meat of your left heel,
how he stuttered apologies,
waited for your strike.
Instead, you called him over,
showed him how to jimmy
the hook out with pliers,
how to tie a blood knot
with two lines.

STEVEN WINN

AFTER SWIMMING

Two boys, slick as eels,
stand shivering
by elevator doors,
shoulders flinching
under taut towel skins.
Panting like hit men
fresh from the deed,
they lean in and
smell it on themselves —
silked hair, chlorine burn,
Doritos dust (Cool Ranch).
Doors slide open,
they step in, ride up,
strip down and
take their turns,
one after the other
pummeled clean.

ANDREEA BOBOC
BRAHMARI'S GIFT

THE DOWNPOUR COMES as a big surprise. Now in its seventh year, the drought in California's San Joaquin Valley has scorched brown patches into lawns, but the unexpected rain startles to life all kinds of creatures. Returning home from the university, I notice a peculiar construction on the spot where the walls above my apartment door come together at an angle. It has the appearance of a longish mud cone or, perhaps, a marine snail shell, though its opening is too small for a snail to pass through.

Soon its inhabitant buzzes out, black-and-yellow, with an impossibly thin waist and wings that shine orange in the sun. It climbs on top of the construction as if to claim it and directs two black orbs at me. My nerves tingle. Is this a wasp? A wasp stung me once, when I was a child, and the insect became tangled in my hair. I still remember my terror at the pulsating, acidic pain, and all for nothing. Bee venom, my mother explained, has at least some therapeutic uses, and you have to feel sorry for the poor insect, who gives up her life with her stinger. Wasp venom, however, is just mean-spirited—the wasp can stab you repeatedly without any peril to itself.

The wasp and I size each other up. I never looked a wasp in the face before. Do insects even have faces? What I see is a hairy boom box, with two black speakers left and right, two orange buttons on the inner side of the speakers, and, in the middle, two gray controls—at least I hope she can be controlled because she looks down at me as if gearing up for an attack, the end of her abdomen arching upward in a warning.

One of the antennae attached to the orange buttons twitches. Was that a wink? I push my glasses back on my nose and take a step closer to peer at the insect. The move proves unwise because the wasp all but lunges at me. Suppressing a shriek, I close my eyes and stand still like a statue. I remember flailing my arms as a little girl and being told this was the reason for being stung in the first place.

This wasp, however, is not needle-happy. Instead, it circles me a few times, buzzing inquisitively. "Oh dear," I say, "how are we going to get along? Don't you see that I live here, too, and that I, too, need to get into my home?" The buzzing stops as if the wasp understands my plea. I open my eyes and look around warily.

Then I look up.

Sure enough, the wasp is perched atop her peculiar construction, her lower body shooting upward like a single pheasant feather. I feel certain that this proud insect is a female. Hmmm, pride comes before the fall. Let's see how proud you look after I call maintenance to destroy your nest. But even as this thought flashes through my mind, a snake of pain lunges from my chest into my left arm, as it's been doing for weeks.

If not destruction, then what?

I figure once I open my door the wasp won't follow me inside. Bees—and, I hope, wasps—rarely pursue someone into darkness, and I have left my blinds and curtains tightly closed to protect my furniture from the sun. How am I to get in, though? Can I distract the insect somehow?

I open my bag, pull out a silk scarf, and unfold it slowly, allowing the sun to amplify its shimmer as I watch the wasp. I feel like a bullfighter distracting his charge. The wasp watches me closely, her lower back stretching upward like an exclamation mark. With leisurely movements, I hide behind the shimmer, covering my hair and neck with the scarf in babushka fashion and shielding my face. There. My vulnerable parts thus armored in silk, I stride the few steps to the door and unlock it. The wasp takes flight again, circling my head. "Sorry," I whisper, "my turn." I fling open my apartment door, get in, and close it in one clumsy move. Only as semi-darkness envelops me do I realize that I have been holding my breath.

My heart is clenching in my chest, and I feel lightheaded. I open the fridge and pour myself a glass of club soda. A piece of chocolate would give me a welcome dopamine rush, but I have cut back on sugar to ward off the indignities of middle age. I feel envious of the insect; her waist looked as slender as a pin. What exactly is she?

I wake up my MacBook and stare at the Google search page. Zoology is not my forte, so I search for the obvious—mud and wasp—and click on images. The screen darkens with black-and-yellow, orangey-and-black, brown-and-black, and electric-blue-and-black wasps.

"Mud daubers," the captions read.

The internet is teeming with mud wasps. I had feared a colony, but all sources reassure me that mud daubers are solitary beings and, overall, quite peaceful. The females of the species do most of the work; they are the ones who build nests out of mud to lay their eggs in. I had been right all along—the wasp is a *she*. A female worker. Something I desperately want to be again and cannot.

NO ONE EVER TOLD ME that grief felt so like a stupor. I read in the *Oxford English Dictionary* that in the Middle Ages stupor meant "loss of physical sensation in a part of the body," something akin to anesthesia, a meaning now obsolete. It doesn't feel obsolete to me. If anything, my stupor has spread. I can doze fitfully for several nights without resting, and then I am plunged into a comatose sleep riddled with nightmares, from which I wake up terrified, not feeling my arms or legs, my heart fluttering with arrhythmia.

"You must let me know if these symptoms persist," my cardiologist says, putting away his stethoscope. His office décor looks antiseptic.

"Takotsubo cardiomyopathy usually resolves on its own, but it's been six weeks, and your left ventricle is still enlarged."

"Should I be worried?"

"Well, I hope not, though I don't like these irregular heartbeats at all. I only see symptoms this drastic in parents who have lost their children. Keep taking your beta blockers. Moderate exercise. And maybe therapy can help with your anxiety and nightmares?"

He's right. I need to talk to someone because my mind has gone, too. Often, I have trouble following what people are saying, and the slightest effort exhausts me. Yesterday I woke up content and stretched in bed for an entire minute before recollection fell on me like a roof caving in on a building.

I've discovered that I can keep at it, though, provided I rest after each task. Every day, I dress in the same outfit (blouse, slacks, sensible shoes, and a merino cardigan for when the air conditioning makes me too cold), then go to the university library, where I pretend to focus on the essay I was working on before everything happened. I read the same paragraphs for a couple of hours, getting up every hour to walk a few steps around the library before I collapse into an armchair. Luckily, because we are on summer break, there are few witnesses.

How am I going to cope, though, when the fall semester starts? To afford grief counseling, I must not only finish my essay but also get it accepted for publication in time for the annual merit raise.

Today, a kind colleague notices me, packs me in her car, and drives me home. At a red light, she feels compelled to offer her sympathies. "He was only nineteen, is that right? How positively dreadful!" She reaches out and squeezes my hand, and I just swallow and nod.

She drops me off, and I slowly climb the twenty feet to my apartment door. I remember the wasp and yesterday's trepidation. Today, I came prepared; I'm wearing a hat.

She's still working on her mud dwelling, but unlike me, she's making progress. A second cone is already finished, and her mandibles are modeling the mud into a third. Could envy shake me out of my stupor? I used to be quite competitive.

"Hello, wasp," I whisper, hoping none of my neighbors can hear me. "If you are going to stay, you need a name. How about Brahmari?" She reminds me of the fierce Indian goddess who defeated her enemies by releasing a cloud of termites, bees, wasps, mosquitos, and spiders over their ranks.

The wasp stops her work and takes her reconnaissance flight around me before she settles down again on her nest, her lower body no longer arched upward. We have gotten used to one another. From under my hat, I wonder: Where does she get the mud from in this heat?

Once indoors, a riptide overwhelms me, and as so often in the past weeks, I need to talk to you. Goldie, do you remember that perpendicular wave that assaulted us on the beach of Golden Gate Park, slapping the phone out of your hand and threatening to drag you into the ocean? How you joked that only Poseidon could pry the phone from your grasp? We laughed even though your Droid was ruined, and you took the battery out and said that if the liquid damage indicator hadn't been activated, they would honor the warranty. We celebrated with ice cream the next day when they exchanged your dead phone for a new one. The guy at the Droid store asked if you dropped your phone in water, and you said no and stared at him with that blue, unflustered gaze of yours that put us all in the poor house whenever we played family poker.

I was your cool aunt—spare mom, you said—your adolescent refuge when parents wouldn't get it, but that day, when our glances high-fived behind the back of the Droid man, I felt apprehensive, as if we knew that this wasn't the universe's last assault on us, that it was only a matter of time before something far more ominous would strike again, and we wouldn't again be so lucky.

What have I been up to in the weeks since you became stardust, you ask? I have been reading *A Grief Observed*. When C. S. Lewis writes that sorrow makes common sense disappear "like an ant in the mouth of a furnace," I feel understood. You, a lover of books, would appreciate the irony of his situation—a Christian apologist calling God the "Cosmic Sadist" and a "spiteful imbecile" after his wife, Joy (another irony), dies of cancer. And there I was, thinking that lethal ironies only applied to you, a vaccinated young man killed by the very disease you were allegedly so well protected against. Now I understand. There is no safety in either faith or science. There is only death.

You have to admire Lewis, though. He complains he cannot work because "grief gives life a permanently provisional feeling," but his writing has never been crisper. If only I could put pen to paper! I started to write you a letter, but Lewis reminds me that "the dead tell us that our mourning does them some kind of wrong. They beg us to stop it."

Stop it how? My reason is too weak to halt the chariot of sorrow, my body weaker still. What Lewis calls "the laziness of grief," that "loathing of the slightest effort," is always with me. Even when my mind fakes normalcy, my afflicted body tells the truth. Stop it how? But even as I ask the question, I know the answer.

I OPEN THE DOOR to check on Brahmari. It's late afternoon, and the heat is gaining. She has stopped working and circles me. After several orbits, she climbs her last unfinished mud cone, flicks her wings, and takes flight directly at my face. I shrink in panic, but curiosity compels me to keep my eyes open. Is this some kind of novel ritual?

Then I understand.

There is no more mud. The soil has become bone-dry again and useless for cone building.

"Brahmari, we have a problem," I say. The wasp stops gyrating and lands on her mud cone, her mandibles working as if with invisible mud. Does she understand me? If we believe the dead want us to stop our mourning, why not believe wasps can comprehend us? In prelapsarian times, talking to animals was commonplace. How else did the serpent persuade Eve to eat of the forbidden fruit?

"I can make mud for you, Brahmari, but it won't be the clay you prefer." The wasp's antennae twitch—she looks as if she's listening.

Back inside, I dump two pounds of apples into a bucket of water. Even in Northern California, outdoor watering has been limited to once a week, but reusing the water in which one washes fruits and vegetables for watering plants is encouraged. This is how I'm going to make a virtue of necessity. After washing the apples, I dump a bunch of carrots into a second container and a pound of potatoes into a third. Would three containers be enough for mud-making?

I bring them all outside. Brahmari plunges into the dirty water like a kingfisher diving for tadpoles. Perched precariously on a floating apple twig, she takes greedy gulps.

This is going to work then. In our shared courtyard, there is a young deciduous tree that has fainted in the heat. Its white flowers are scattered about, and its leaves are drooping on its branches. I drizzle the dirty water around its trunk, making sure there is no runoff. I follow up with a second container. And the third. The wasp circles me, buzzing deliriously.

I am rain.

I haul the containers back upstairs. There are no more veggies to wash, but I could wipe down my apartment. The "laziness of grief" has allowed plenty of dust to gather, and dust combines with water into mud.

I fill a few more containers with dirty water and haul them downstairs, carefully pouring them around the trunk of the youngster. The parched soil guzzles insatiably, allowing no mud to form, but the wasp circles closer, as if urging me to keep at it.

More water! What else can I wash? My entrance door looks dusty, and all my windowsills need a good scrubbing. Three more buckets of dirty water, then.

Finally, mud! I stagger back into my apartment, faint with exhaustion. This is the first night I don't need a pill to knock me out, the first night I don't seek comfort in *A Grief Observed*. The moment my head hits the pillow, I sink into a shapeless sleep.

THE NEXT MORNING, the wasp is back at work. The young tree looks alert. I feel as if I had the flu: every muscle in my body aches.

Luna, the lady who looks after me, finds me midday in a groaning heap.

"¡Ay, señora! ¿Qué más pasó?"

Más is one way to put it.

My Spanish is not good enough to explain about the wasp, and there is only so much a housekeeper can take. For years, she has put up with my love of indoor spiders, suppressing her instinct to tear down their webs and send them packing. A story about how I'm helping a wasp build a mud cone would make me more eccentric in her eyes than I can afford. Luckily, when she arrives, the wasp is nowhere to be seen, and Luna doesn't notice the mud cones, which I camouflaged with a tall plant I had delivered. What she sees instead is that the apartment sparkles, and I left her with nothing to do. I stumble over my apology in Spanish, but she dismisses it with praise.

"¡Qué bueno que haya hecho un poco de ejercicio!" Then she asks innocently, "¿Tal vez, señora, le gustaría que yo limpiara la telaraña de Carlotta?"

We chuckle, drink coffee, and she chops down the pile of veggies I washed the day before. Luna has baptized all my spiders Carlotta and, with a twinkle in her eye, presented me on my fiftieth birthday with a plank of wood engraved with the words *Aquí se permite que vivan las arañas* to immortalize my edict of amnesty.

Because I focus on each sentence as I speak it, companionship does not feel as oppressive in Spanish as it does in English. But jollity feels blasphemous. Sometimes I catch Luna watching me out of the corner of her eye and shaking her head. Before she leaves, she bakes her formidable apple pie: double-crusted, with cinnamon and raisins. I force her to take half of it home for her family.

Alone again, my old exhaustion returns. The muscle strain worsens, and grief wrestles me back to bed. A creature presses on my chest and wiggles its way into my left arm, though not as painfully as before. What if I pretended that takotsubo doesn't refer to my broken heart but to its other meaning, the earthen vessel used by Japanese fishermen to trap octopuses in the ocean? I saw it on YouTube. The octopus is a brilliant escape artist, though, so there is hope for my mind's release from the tentacles of my grieving body.

I reach for Lewis, but my hand grabs a book on medieval sloth by mistake. I am back to laziness even though I know that work is my only salvation. Perhaps this book can help me with my article?

It can't, but it speaks so uncannily to my current situation that I sit up in bed. I read that, at the beginning of medieval times, *acedia* used to mean spiritual dryness—a diminishing faith in God—but by the late Middle Ages, it became secularized to laziness proper. Intellectuals, especially, were suspected of *acedia* because, unlike physical labor, mental work was often invisible.

If sloth has been my destiny so far, this "laziness of grief" isn't insuperable. There are obstructions ahead, though. St. Augustine warns we can get too attached to our grief: "I carried my bloody and lacerated soul when it was unwilling to be carried by me. I found no place where I could put it down."

Could I at least put my grief to work, the lazy kind?

I remember yesterday's dust and dirt and feel hopeful. In my need, I had turned to dust, not to perish but to survive. Grief has unmoored me; mud has restored me.

TODAY, I'm not pretending to work in the library. I am staying home, doing Anne Lamott's "prone yoga," during which "you just lay around as much as possible." I might coin my own version, writer's prone yoga, which means that I write my article from before Goldie died while I lie in bed. No title yet, but I'll have to incorporate *Everyman*, the medieval play that sits at its center. My energy does not suffice for both sitting up and writing, so I prop myself up on pillows, necessity, and envy.

Speaking of envy, Brahmari has quit building and is now hunting spiders, which she doesn't kill but tranquilizes with her stinger to serve as a supply of fresh food for her newborn larvae. Next, I read, she will seal her mud cones with the larvae and the paralyzed spiders inside, allowing the new wasps to pupate and fend for themselves. How did I miss the part about the killing of spiders the first time around?

Yesterday, I saw Brahmari skulking backward into one of her mud cones, stunned spider between her mandibles. I want to believe the spider was a black widow, my least favorite, but I cannot be sure. So the news is that my tireless architect has become an assassin.

I read that to feed her offspring, one single wasp might tranquilize up to five hundred spiders. Five hundred! I fear for Carlotta and her ilk. *Aquí ya no se permite que vivan las arañas.* I vexed Nature by aiding and abetting a serial killer. Did I really, though? I try to remember if it was Shakespeare who said that when we use art to interfere with nature, "the art itself is nature," but the effort exhausts me.

When I open my front door, Brahmari unexpectedly flies in. I see Carlotta run to the edge of her web and then hide in a mask on the wall while Brahmari circles my living room as if on spider patrol. For some reason, this infuriates me. I grab a kitchen towel and wave it in her face.

"Shoo!" I yell. "Get away from my spider!" I feel my anger rise above my fear. If she's going to sting me for this, so be it.

The wasp stops, uncertain, in midair, as if reassessing our relationship. Her rainmaker, who helped her achieve her biological purpose, is

ANDREEA BOBOC **43**

preventing her from fulfilling it. I see her back arch again as if gearing up for a fight. Or is it a question?

"No," I say, "we are not partners in crime. The spider sacrifice you must accomplish on your own. Get out!"

I drop my towel, ready to face her venom, but she flies out. I close the door and keep an eye out for Carlotta. Half an hour later, when I see her emerge from her hiding place and settle again in her silk hammock, I breathe a sigh of relief.

I cut myself a piece of Luna's pie. The first bite used to taste like a sinner's heaven, but grief stifles even the aroma of freshly baked apples. I pause my fork, unsure if this diminished experience is worth the calories, but weakling that I am, I convince myself I need the sugar to focus.

My concentration is soon broken. There is a faint tap on the door, followed by the sound of rustling paper. Have they increased my rent again? Now I really do need that raise. No, this is just a note saying that all entryways will be swept clean by maintenance, and that we should remove all obstructing objects.

Oh, goody. Should I turn in the spider killer? I am an angry rainmaker but also a practical one. There is no telling how many spiders she's tranquilized and stored already, so their sacrifice would be in vain. But more daubers would mean fewer spiders and, therefore, more pests . . .

I make my way to the maintenance office. The manager comes out to greet me. He is short and stocky, with kind eyes. His brother is Luna's husband, who went all the way to Mexico City to court her and persuade her to come and live among whacky gringos who keep spiders as pets.

"Teacher! I was sorry to hear about your nephew. I know you loved him very much."

I nod to push down the lump in my throat. He lowers his head for a moment before he looks at me.

"But good to see you are busy again. I noticed your polished entryway. Looks like you did a lot of work on it recently."

"Thank you. I just rearranged my plants and was wondering.... Could you skip me just this once when you send out your cleaning crew?"

He scratches his head. "I also noticed you got some mud dauber cones on the exterior wall."

Damn. The camouflage has failed.

"Kinda incredible that a wasp could find the mud to build them in this weather. Are you sure you don't want those taken down? If you do nothing, you will get more. Once the daubers find a safe place, they keep coming back to their old nests."

"I am sure. I kinda like them there."

He smiles. "Okay, then. At any rate, you might have finally solved your spider problem. Luna tells me she's been trying to rid you of them for ages."

BACK IN MY APARTMENT I wonder if perhaps grief has shrunk my imagination. Mud daubers have existed since long before I met Brahmari. How long? The internet sources don't say. But surely, I am not Brahmari's rainmaker any more than she is mine. By enlisting me to help her, she helped me put my grief to work. Even better: I've started to write again.

So my anger is misplaced. Once, in an Edinburgh Airbnb, I befriended a tuxedo cat named Pirate. He jumped on the counter while I was making a salad, sniffed at my butter lettuce, and became so concerned that I couldn't feed myself properly that he went out in the Scottish rain and caught a sparrow. He laid it, barely twitching, on the carpet at my feet. Perhaps Brahmari is like that cat, attempting to rid me of spiders while supporting her offspring. We had been in this together from the beginning; it was me who let her down, not the other way round.

I feel contrite for not having considered "the idea that I, or any mortal at any time, may be utterly mistaken as to the situation he is really in." More C. S. Lewis. Perhaps a peace offering would reconcile me with Brahmari. What do mud daubers eat besides insects? Honey?

I can only find a honeydew in my pantry. Luna must have brought it, together with the other shopping. I cut a slice and leave it out in front of my entrance, close to the potted plant, checking on it throughout the afternoon. A family of ants enjoys it, but there is no trace of Brahmari.

I go to bed more dejected than usual. Even with the nightly delta breeze, it is brutally hot. The air conditioning whooshes me to sleep.

In the darkness, I recognize the set of *Everyman*, the morality play I am working on. Here is the raised place for God, and over there the houses for Everyman's friends and relatives, all of whom abandon him on his pilgrimage to meet Death. Aside from my character, the professor, there are five actors onstage, though not the ones I expect. My heart is pounding.

The Professor:	What's happening? Why am I here?
Wisdom:	To understand that life is mere interpretation and, therefore, an illusion. Death is the only reality.
Change:	Not so. I am the only reality.
Buddha:	What Change means is you can't seek permanence in impermanent things.
The Professor:	Then what shall I do?
Change:	Embrace me. You look like you need a hug.
Epictetus:	Remember that you are merely playing a part according to the will of the Director. So play it well, and don't ask why. Only the Director knows why.
Lewis:	He calls himself the Director now? That spiteful imbecile!

I wish the Director would appear to make sense of all this. Nobody comes. I hear Goldie calling in the distance: "Don't listen to them, Auntie! I'm okaaay!"

I am flooded with relief.

A wave demolishes the set. Actors and scaffolding disappear under water.

I gasp awake; my left arm hurts, asleep.

It is a little after 7:00 a.m., and the temperature is already in the seventies, but I shiver as I change from pajamas into house clothes. Work. I need work.

I carry a bowl of dirty fruit water downstairs to the young tree, whose smallish crown resembles a green fist against the sky. Because of the drought, tap water smells funny. I pour it around the tree, where it hits the soil as it would pavement.

I feel physically weighed down, as if I aged overnight. I am fifty-three years old, but I climb the stairs to my apartment as if I were ninety, gasping for breath and holding onto the banister. I check on my potted plant, the mud dauber camouflage. As I part the leaves to feel the soil, I gulp. There, between two clumps of earth, lies Brahmari, her antennae barely twitching.

Sorrow feels like a myocardial contusion. Wasn't she supposed to live through the summer and deliver two generations of daubers? There is a drop of water still clinging to my bowl. I aim it at her head and soak her. No reaction. I pick her up and put her on my palm.

"Brahmari, don't die!" I whisper. "I will give you honeydew if you live." Can one do CPR on a wasp? I stroke her body as gently as I can.

For a good while, she just lies there, an occasional twitch of her legs the only indication of life. But minutes later she gets up and starts to groom her antennae. I read somewhere that insects remove various chemicals this way to enhance their hearing. Or maybe she's just wiping off the water I threw in her face.

Finally, she returns to her old self. In fact, she looks indestructible. I am so elated I don't realize I hold a live wasp in my hand. And then the same pulsating, acidic pain I felt as a little girl sets my palm on fire. I shake Brahmari off, but the pain doesn't overwhelm my feeling of relief. A sting is light punishment for contemplating treason.

After I tend to my swelling hand, I return outside to admire her finished work: three mud cones, all sealed in anticipation of offspring. The last cone is bicolored, my gift of mud clearly visible. I seal my own work in an envelope to send it out: twenty pages of literary criticism wrestled from the maw of grief. Brahmari's gift. ◆

GEORGE CHOUNDAS

BECAUSE YOU DIDN'T ASK, DEPUTY, IS WHAT PAUL SAID (BEFORE HE GOT ARRESTED FOR ACCESSORY TO MURDER)

MY FRIEND Paul Kim lives on a lake in middle Georgia. It's called Lake Oconee. There's a lake just south of Lake Oconee, cut off from it by a single dam. It's called Lake Sinclair.

Lake Sinclair allows boathouses, but Lake Oconee prohibits them. Sinclair residents own to the waterline, Oconee residents only up to the yellow markers because the lakefront is technically the property of Georgia Power. These facts notwithstanding, Sinclair's property values are fifteen or twenty percent lower than Oconee's. Sinclair is the one where, years ago, they kept finding all the corpses with the mangled feet.

Another difference between the two bodies of water is the imaginary line of latitude that runs between them, right at Wallace Dam. That line, administered by the state forestry commission, marks the northern boundary of the alligator's natural habitat. Oconee homeowners who go for a swim and spot the flickering yellow eyes of an alligator can call the commission and have it caught and removed. Sinclair homeowners who go for a swim and spot the flickering yellow eyes of an alligator can swim faster. They can also tell their friends. But they can't call the commission. Or, more precisely, they can, but after placing the call, they'll only learn they've purchased property south of the habitat line. There, the alligators must be left alone to live as they see fit.

The commission looked into the Sinclair corpses. It concluded that only an alligator with training or a fetish would so consistently, and so exclusively, maul the right foot of its victims. Shortly after ruling out alligator attacks, the commission received a report from a recreational diver about a spike in the lake floor, pointed like a needle but stout in the shaft.

Sinclair's black water, I said to Paul. Maybe two or three feet of visibility. How's a diver spotting anything on the lake floor?

I didn't know what I was talking about. I don't dive. I just wanted to know if Paul knew what he was talking about.

Early morning, Paul said, no wakes, you can see ten or twelve feet. This guy was muck diving. Buzzing the lakebed to see what he could see. And he saw. This is what Paul said.

The commission deployed its own divers. These quickly found three other spikes of identical shape and dimension. Then, during a joint survey with the state bureau of investigation, the divers found a corpse— or some proportion of one—still spiked through its right foot to the lakebed.

That's when Paul told me, with a kind of conspiratorial relish, that the alligators caught in Oconee are relocated to Sinclair. This is the most efficient outcome for the commission's personnel, as it minimizes the distance traveled with a dangerous creature. The commission has no elaborate repositioning protocol. There is no crane, no mobile aquarium. The commission's default conveyance is a pickup truck outfitted with a cage, and its staff prefer not to drive with an unwilling passenger for longer than they have to. Relocation to Sinclair is also the least disruptive outcome for the alligator, Sinclair's ecosystem being functionally indistinguishable from Oconee's.

The lake-to-lake relocation program is kept quiet, very quiet. It was Paul's downlake neighbor, Ingram Respess, who told Paul about it. Respess knew because he worked at the commission, up until he was arrested for the murders. Two gentlemen from the bureau paid Paul a visit and asked him if he'd ever observed Respess do anything suspicious, and Paul said, Other than have two last names? But the gentlemen didn't enjoy jokes, and didn't like no any better, so they asked Paul to recount every interaction he'd ever had with Respess. Mostly hi and bye is what Paul could remember, and only two conversations all told.

The first was when Paul had ambled over to Respess's home with a bottle of wine. Paul couldn't find a corkscrew and thought he'd borrow one. But Respess didn't have one, and so Respess tried to push the cork down or score it into pieces, but none of that worked.

Finally, Paul told Respess to keep the wine and open it at his leisure, and Respess joked it was like a housewarming gift—because it was the first time Paul and Respess had met, even though Respess had bought the house months earlier and had been living there three weeks—and Paul joked it was like he was assigning Respess homework. Paul left Respess with the wine and smiling.

Their only other conversation was when they had chatted about Respess's job, about the commission, about how friends and family of commission personnel who made it known they were considering buying property on Sinclair were invariably warned off by their commission connections, about how these friends and family then learned that Sinclair was not only gator-friendly but gator-stocked, and about how these disclosures happened often enough that a growing population of middle Georgia landowners who had nearly bought on Sinclair, and of realtors who had been briefed by their clients on the reason for their deciding not to buy on Sinclair, were getting wind of the protocol.

Neither conversation shed light on why Respess had stapled his victims to the lake bed, or exactly how he'd managed this, or whether they'd been alive or dead when he'd done so—the lungs and their evidence long gone—or whether the unusual modus was to service some ritualistic preoccupation or just to hide the corpses until enough time had passed for the bones and tissue of the foot to deteriorate around the spike and finally release them to the surface and notoriety. If the latter, Respess clearly had miscalculated and believed they would loosen and surface only after years—perhaps even only after his own death—rather than mere months. But the only thing dumber than not knowing is speculating like you know when you don't. I'll stop.

Paul hadn't liked the way the investigators asked their vinegar questions, or looked at everything except him while asking them, or called him Mister Paul, which suggested they maybe thought his first name was Kim. So Paul had waited until after the investigators wrapped up. He had waited until after one of them asked a genius masterwork of a question about whether there was anything else they should know, until after the other had handed him a business card like a monarch bestowing a ruby-cosseted pearl on a peasant (Cosseted? I said to Paul, and he said, It's a word, isn't it?, and I shrugged and said, Sometimes you make up words, and he said, No, I don't, and I said, Sometimes stories, too, and he said, Not this one, and I don't make up stories, stories make themselves up, and I left it there, because he was hungry, and Paul gets petulant when he's hungry), until after both investigators had walked out of his door and onto his porch and off of his porch.

I guess, Paul called out his front door, neither of you deputies cares to know what Respess used to try to open that wine.

The investigators turned and stared and stared.

I guess, Paul said to me, state investigators don't much like being called deputy.

Paul was released from the Greene County Jail after twenty-four hours. Even in middle Georgia, insolence isn't a crime. Respess is serving life at Hancock State Prison. When non-alligator humans do it, slaughter is murder.

I guess, I said to Paul, you knew what you were saying when you said it.

Respess's house shows no sign of sale or activity. Respess still owns it from prison, so far as Paul knows. They've found more spikes than corpses. But Respess isn't talking.

Paul likes to say the families of Sinclair live on its shores in a kind of pretty oblivion.

They pretend not to mind the alligators. They pretend not to believe the rumors of alligator shuttles. And this is why with each passing year,

Paul surmises, they never let themselves notice, let alone consider, when after sunset they stare and stare into the dark, the more and more points of yellow staring back. ◆

NICK RATTNER

TWO SKETCHES OF KENJI

It was fun to find the day still
soft under strawberries'
green roofs, bitten free
and spat into a plastic bag
slung over the corner
of a cabinet. It was glory
to wash your face in the sink
in the hall with no mirror
above it and call that
devotion. It was easy to
make nothing of ourselves
so nothing should ever
stand in our way.

Your armpits glowed
with last night's hash.
Last night's gin & tonics
became orange blossoms
in your morning sweat
and the only flowers
you ever pressed
your nose to were lilies
on a polyester mattress
for which you never had a sheet.

SAM MOE

LATE NIGHT

You are in his bathroom again, sitting on the tub's cold edge, marveling at his wife's efficiency, the way she hung gold and silver stars on the ceiling, the tinsel lining the doorway, someone's drunken lipstick kiss on the mirror. You wore blue on a whim, painted wings on the backs of your hands, just in case you wanted to fly away. Your shoes hurt, your cigarette is burned down to the heat. They had horses at the wedding. They have a red refrigerator. You open the window and look out at New York City.

STELLA WONG

SMOKIN

after courbet's l'origine du monde

and you live
here with bare
walls like you

are an ass-
sassin of
the order

derived from
hashish smoke,
speaking of

which. the old
sequoias
caught on   fire

including
the second
tallest in

the world. it's
easy   to
cry   over.

natural
underline.
getting pub-

lic serviced.
expose wood.
underbrush

for saplings
to grow. we
didn't see

mother   bears
nor cubs. I
can't call you

cute but hot
is okay.
death might break

a new rec-
ord in the
valley to-

day. escape
the concert-
ed effort.

MOLLIE SWAYNE

COWBOY

I came home
from the movies
at the time of day
where you don't need
to turn on the lights quite yet
everything is dim, dusk
has started indoors
and will soon seep outside
to the porch
it is so quiet I can hear
my neighbor's air conditioner
I try to enjoy the freedom
of my thoughts, be a real
cowboy about them
I try to enjoy the present
in a way that is not
preemptive future remembering
the other day at Chipotle
when the girl
gave me my cup
she set it on the counter
and made the noise movies make
when an angel descends from heaven:
an *ahhhhhh!*
with vibrato
I picked up the cup
and did it back to her:
ahhhhhh!
then I said
"I don't know why I did that"
but of course

I am a true cowboy
at heart
I love
the red horizon
the sweet smell
of grass
the glory
of it all
amen

"I try to enjoy the freedom of my thoughts" is adapted from a line from
Baek Sehee's therapist in *I Want to Die but I Want to Eat Tteokbokki: A
Memoir*.

FINOLA DAVIDSON
BEHIND

LORENE ISN'T EVEN DRINKING when she makes the bet. Two minutes before the virtual happy hour, she pours her roommate's extra-pulp orange juice into a jam jar—if anyone asks, it's a screwdriver—and pads to her bedroom. Abdomen throbbing, she shakes four acetaminophen gel caps from the plastic bottle sitting open on her desk and washes them down.

And shudders. Extra-pulp is *way* too much texture.

When she opens her laptop, the email from Alexis fills the screen. She clicks the link. A preview box pops up, displaying a low-resolution Lorene and asking whether she wants to join with or without video. She shifts the laptop left, to hide nail holes the last tenant left in the wall, and wipes shine from her nose. After last month's electricity bill hit $197, she and the roommates agreed to keep the house a toasty 80 degrees. At least Lorene's hair is too limp to frizz.

Adjustments made, she should feel better. But dread and cramps fill her belly. She buttons her shirt to the neck, tucks her Saint Sebastian medal inside, and joins with video.

The happy hour's in gallery view. Alexis looms, face framed by caramel hair and fabric frothing up from her milky blouse; Lorene checks Alexis's throat, but if she's wearing the charm necklace, ruffles hide it. Other heads bob in smaller boxes stacked beside Alexis. The black splotch in the corner of Lorene's screen, from when she knocked her laptop off the bed last month, half-swallows her own image.

Every time Alexis summons the old team, Lorene fantasizes Alexis will admit regrets, grovel, cry. Every time, gallery view tells Lorene she's an optimistic dolt. It's like they're still on the bus, Alexis holding court behind Coach Pearl's back, while—

Lorene twitches, flicking the memory away. As Alexis talks, full of chill rhythm and vocal fry (*half-marathon in Brooklyn, fun trip for you guys*), Lorene catalogs the heads. No Tara. Of course, no Iffy.

"—can't host you on race weekend, but you can split an Airbnb." Alexis props her chin on her fist. On her forearm glint gold hairs, all lying flat in one direction, like she combed them. "Don't unmute. Just give me a thumbs-up if yes."

Thumbs wave in every box but Lorene's.

"Why not, Lorene?" Alexis coos.

Lorene's appointment with the OB/GYN is in November. It'll cost $350 minimum. She can't afford a trip or another registration fee. She can't imagine admitting that to Alexis.

Another registration fee. That's her excuse. She unmutes. "I'm running a marathon at the end of October. I'll be in recovery."

"You're running a marathon?" Alexis laughs. "Sorry, it's just, you were always weaker over longer distances. What was your 5K again?"

It might be the cramps, or gallery view, or Iffy. Lorene should leave it but doesn't. "My last marathon, I missed qualifying for Chicago by nine seconds."

"Your last marathon?" Alexis looks offended. With a trepidatious flush of pleasure, Lorene grasps Alexis has never run one. "When?"

"Right after in-person marathons opened up again."

"A while ago, huh? Let's make it fun. A hundred bucks says you can't beat your PR."

An alien impulse surges in Lorene, snaking through her pain and nausea, up her throat, into her tongue. She swigs orange juice to silence herself. She swallows. Pulp stuck in her molars, she blurts, "Two hundred says I qualify for Boston."

After a pause, Alexis flashes whitened teeth. "When you lose, Venmo me."

THEY WEREN'T SUPPOSED TO WEAR jewelry to meets. But Alexis, who made varsity freshman year, never removed her charm necklace—as if her head would tumble off without it, like the girl with the velvet ribbon in the fairytale. The JV runners competed to buy charms for her. If she liked what you gave her, you could sit near her on the bus.

Lorene saved up from bagging groceries at Food Lion and spent hours selecting a gilded filigree racehorse from the affordable options on Etsy. The package came on a Saturday. On Monday, Lorene asked to use the bathroom with five minutes left in last-period Spanish. She arrived early to the scuffed track beside the school and fidgeted, racehorse clamped in a sweaty fist. Alexis always showed up ten minutes before practice and did plyometric exercises on the grass till boys started hooting at her through the windows of buses peeling from the curb.

Alexis jogged up right on time. "Hi, Lauren."

"Lorene," Lorene said.

"Didn't I say that?" Alexis dropped into a clapping push-up.

"I got this for you." Lorene turned her back on the flagpole, hiding from any kid who might glance out across the athletic fields, and opened her fingers. The racehorse winked in a frozen frisk across her lifeline.

Alexis popped upright and plucked the charm from Lorene's hand. "Is it fourteen-carat gold?"

It was gold-plated stainless steel. "Oh, I, I'm not sure."

"I can only wear fourteen-carat. I'm allergic to impure metals. They turn my neck green." Alexis held out the racehorse.

Numbly, Lorene took it back. "I didn't realize."

"No worries. Hey." Alexis peered at Lorene's chest. "What's that?"

Lorene touched her sternum. Her fingers brushed a dime-sized metal wafer, pierced at the top and threaded on a fragile chain. On the wafer was etched, needle-fine, a man shot through with arrows.

Lorene's mom was a Protestant so nondenominational she didn't go to church. Most nights, she read the Bible in her easy chair, a Coors cracked open in the cupholder, her way to unwind after a twelve-hour shift at the warehouse. But Lorene's dad had been Italian Catholic. For their honeymoon—way back when he made good money, before the accident, the oxycodone, and the final overdose after Lorene's sixth birthday—they spent three days in Rome. He bought the wafer from a souvenir hawker near some famous marble fountain. Lorene's mom gave it to Lorene when she turned seven. "Don't lose it," Mom had said.

Lorene stored the wafer in her locker during practice, but that day she'd forgotten, rushing to catch Alexis alone. "Saint Sebastian. He's, um, the patron saint of athletes."

Alexis leaned forward. Warm, minty breath struck Lorene's skin. "Are those knives?"

"Arrows."

"Morbid." Alexis straightened up and fixed Lorene with a bright stare.

After a moment, Lorene understood that Alexis was expecting her to offer up Saint Sebastian in place of the deficient racehorse. She imagined sitting on the bus behind Alexis and her friends forever, hearing them laugh, not joining in. She imagined telling Mom she'd lost the wafer, bracing for the look that would crack across Mom's hard-boned face.

"It's—it's just copper," Lorene said. "The gold's gilt."

"Are you sure?"

"It's not allergies," a voice said behind Lorene—a weird voice, gruff yet girlish. Iffy. Lorene, startled, clutched her throat.

"What's that, Cousin It?" Alexis asked.

Iffy stepped into Lorene's peripheral vision, a tall blur with long, lank hair. "When metal turns your skin green, that's not allergies. It's a chemical reaction."

Alexis trilled a laugh. "I think I know my own body. Like, I know what I'm allergic to."

Iffy said nothing. Lorene stared at the grass.

Alexis snorted and turned away. "Whatever."

After practice, in a locker-room bathroom stall, Lorene jerked out the day's eighth oversaturated tampon. It dangled blood-gorged, big as a rat on its string. She fumbled the racehorse from her pocket, threaded it onto the string, and mummified charm and tampon with toilet paper. The mummy she interred in the trash box screwed to the stall wall. She wanted to forget her talk with Alexis had happened. She wanted to forget Iffy, skulking behind them, witnessing.

Some teams rode to meets in air-conditioned buses rented specially, but Lorene's team rode a rusty yellow short bus. Their opponents called them, inventively, The Retards. Alexis sat in front, one row behind Coach Pearl, a stern blond dental hygienist whose mysterious love life the seniors whispered about during warm-up jogs. Girls acceptable to Alexis jostled for seats near her. Four empty rows separated them from Tara, whose dropout brother dealt weed to half the school. Lorene sat behind Tara. Iffy sat behind Lorene. Because there was someone behind Lorene, when Alexis texted the team's group chat, *Hey WT do you recognize your daddy* or *have indoor plumbing* or *know how to insert tampons*, Lorene could be pretty sure *WT* wasn't her.

WT meant white trash. Alexis abbreviated in case Coach Pearl saw her phone.

The tampon text was Lorene's fault. One period she'd been rationing. She'd remembered stashing extra Kotex under the bathroom sink, but when she checked, they were gone. Mom had just paid rent and gotten the Kia repaired. Lorene, having blown her savings on a stupid charm, couldn't ask for money. So: she'd grab a handful of tampons from the school nurse's office and make them last till her Friday paycheck. But even using the super-absorbent kind she worried would give her toxic shock, she bled through fast.

Before her first period, culture had promised menstruation would usher her into empowered womanhood—or at least lend her an abject glamor, like Carrie at prom. But she ended up feeling about her period how she would feel about sex when she finally dared to have it with a glum coworker at her second job out of college. What had been billed as a life-defining moment turned out painful, wet, and smelly.

So there she was, on the bus, spotting through her panties. The bus was stuffy, the windows closed. When the girls breathed, they breathed in the plastic seat covers, the grooved metal floor, cheap flowery deodorants, sweat. Now, a salty odor rose from Lorene's lap. She breathed through her mouth and told herself no one would notice.

Her phone buzzed. *Hey WT what smells like SHRIMP???*

Lorene slid down in her seat, thighs pressed together. Iffy was right behind her. Could she sniff out that it was Lorene leaking? Would she defend herself, name the real culprit?

A hand pushed forward between the window and Lorene's seat-back. Dazed by horror, she fixated on the fingernails, each clipped to raw quick on the sides and rising to a sharp white point in the middle. Belatedly, she decoded the pink-wrapped oblong the hand was holding. *Thank you, Jesus.*

When she snatched the tampon, she rattled the hand's knuckles against the window. "Sorry," she whispered. "Thanks."

The hand withdrew.

Lorene was already scheming how to sneak to a bathroom at the meet. She didn't consider speaking up to Alexis for Iffy—didn't consider admitting or explaining. It wouldn't occur to her till years later that Iffy might have hoped she would.

LORENE'S NEXT RUN, Iffy joins her.

It's intervals that day: eight miles at recovery pace, five 600-meter sprints mixed in. Lorene's alarm goes off an hour before sunrise. If she sleeps any later, she won't have time to shower and blow-dry before work. She brews coffee in the run-down kitchen, dominated by a dirty-white stove whose dials cock a few degrees off true. She gulps a cup at the pocked yellow counter, swallows two more acetaminophen, laces her Ghosts, and slips into the humid dark.

She jogs down her street, giant magnolias dwarfing the houses, and turns onto the main road. Across the overpass. Past the gym advertising Pilates, the taqueria with the life-sized plastic cow on the roof. Past the nicer houses and better-groomed trees, the Montessori school, the café with the fresh cardamom churros, the dilapidated plaza with the Food Lion two times bigger than the one where Lorene worked in high school. Already, the air is balmy. Lorene's underarms are greasing, her scalp sprouting moist itches. She checks her heart rate on her secondhand Garmin. Too high. She slows till she feels like she's bouncing in place.

Something pokes her up between the legs. The stem of her menstrual cup. She forgot to dump it before she left. Now, it's making itself known.

Lorene bought the cup with the first paycheck from her new job. She'd been reading articles in online women's magazines about how reusables saved you money in the long run, whereas disposables, with their chlorine bleaches, their chemical dyes, and their artificial fragrances, trashed the environment and seeped toxins into your bloodstream through your most intimate membranes. Clicking checkout on the cup made Lorene feel responsible and clean. The shine wore off when the cup's ¼ and ½ oz markers proved it wasn't in her head; she really did bleed like a stuck sow—or suffer "menorrhagia," per WebMD. Her paycheck didn't come with health insurance, but Wikipedia said menorrhagia could be a warning sign for cancers, infections, and hormonal syndromes that cause infertility. She found an OB/GYN who took patients without insurance and scheduled an appointment for November, far enough in the future that she could save money for the appointment by cutting other spending.

The episode cast a pall. Not that Lorene regrets realizing the problem, but hey, trade-offs. And she hates dumping the cup after runs.

Up-and-down motion foams the blood. Even when she flips the cup over the toilet and shakes, lacy red bubbles stick to the silicone.

At the graveyard intersection, the clouds have begun to blush over the black trees. She trots toward a hill budding tombstones like teeth. A smoky whiteness smudges the side of her vision. She swipes her eye.

The smudge elongates, growing a head, arms, hands, fingers peaking in short points.

Lorene's heart bucks. She bolts along the sidewalk bordering the graveyard, but the smudge tails her, gaining color and definition. Its sluicing hair tints wan brown, its face wan gray. From its translucent thigh streams a wan red ribbon.

Lorene sprints faster than her best 800, her best 400. She whips by the graveyard. As the sidewalk curves upward, the smudge throws out an arm. A fingernail grazes Lorene's neck. Something tugs her throat and slithers down her chest.

When Lorene crests the hill, a breeze blows in. The smudge disintegrates.

Lorene stumbles to a stop, ribs heaving, cup's stem scraping painfully, and pulls at her sweaty shirt collar. Saint Sebastian lies in a pool of broken chain between her breasts, fall halted by her sports bra's chest band.

She wonders whether Iffy meant to break it. She wonders how Iffy can haunt her when Iffy didn't die.

LORENE FINISHED her high school's required science curriculum junior year. The guidance counselor, a granny-looking lady with stone chips for eyes, told her four years of science gave her a better shot at a college scholarship, so Lorene signed up for the semester-long senior electives on offer. In the spring, that was Anatomy with the biology teacher, a hapless pipe cleaner of a woman named Ms. Joyner. Thirteen boys took Anatomy and only two girls, Lorene and Iffy. Ms. Joyner seemed to consider the girls each other's natural allies, under the circumstances. She put them together in her seating chart and paired them on projects.

Lorene and Iffy didn't speak. Lorene glanced between the projector screen and her notebook, where she copied the slides in finger-cramping script. Iffy, bulking to her left, pressed letters into her paper that did not add up to words. She sketched faces from odd angles: three-quarters profile, up the nose, overhead, behind. She drew clustered symbols, hashtags, dollar signs, ampersands, like she was inventing a code. Toward the end of class, she would scribble over her letters, sketches, and symbols till they became indented smudges.

Inevitably, Ms. Joyner paired Lorene and Iffy for the fetal pig dissection. 50% of the grade was based on notetaking and a final lab report.

"How about," Lorene said to the air between their desks, "I take notes. You dissect."

Iffy dissected. The pig bloomed across their tray: Glasgow smile, Y-incision, groin parted, skin peeled back in petals. Lorene's fingers stained ink-blue while Iffy's latex gloves mottled red. Five minutes before the bell, Iffy cleaned the instruments and stowed the tray.

Lorene doesn't remember seeing Iffy palm the scalpel.

That weekend, the team had a meet. All the seniors had made varsity, but that didn't change the seating arrangements on the bus: Alexis behind Coach Pearl, coterie sticking close, Tara behind the coterie, Lorene behind Tara, Iffy behind Lorene.

Lorene's partial college scholarship depended on her "maintaining academic standards" till graduation. This vague, terrifying requirement had her studying like John Stuart Mill. She sat with a beat-up Anatomy textbook across her knees. In diagrams, the body's arteries made a red stick figure with frills. She was tracing arteries with a finger, mouthing *carotid, pulmonary, thoracic, hepatic, gastric, renal, femoral*, when a hiss sounded behind her. Like someone hosing down a tarp. Liquid hitting her seatback.

Alexis twisted around. "Are you *peeing* back there?" she hollered.

A raw, beachy smell hit Lorene. Baffled, she glanced down at her dry lap. Blood was flowing along the floor's metal grooves toward her heels.

AFTER WORK, Lorene searches "Iffy Bullock" online. Iffy didn't die on the bus; the scalpel only nicked the artery in her thigh, and Coach Pearl twisted her shirt into a tourniquet while Lorene sat staring forward, legs frozen in a calf-raise so blood didn't soak her socks. Iffy could've died later—but would she haunt *Lorene*? Lorene's never supposed she mattered enough to anyone to provoke a haunting.

She googles around for an obituary. She scours Instagram and Facebook. On LinkedIn she unearths an Iffy Hawkins. Did Iffy get married, change her name? This Hawkins person graduated from UNC-Chapel

Hill and is attending medical school at the Uniformed Services University of Health Sciences in Bethesda. Her profile picture shows a woman in a baseball cap and aviators, jaw outthrust.

Does a frisson strike Lorene at the thin mouth, the knifing nose? Of course not. When did young Lorene look anyone in the face?

For the next three months, Lorene runs a hillier route rather than pass the graveyard. As the weeks pass, the daylight contracts. Temperatures boil, plunge, freeze, and climb back into the tepid 50s. Pine needles rust on the sidewalks. Pumpkins sprout from porches. Witches and skeletons dangle from front-yard branches; orange fairy lights spangle eaves. Meanwhile, Lorene tries to save money. She eats oatmeal, peanut butter, rice, beans. She portions out her Gatorade powder and GU gels. She puts 600-plus miles on her Ghosts and senses, from her twinging left knee, that she should buy a new pair, but she puts it off, off, off, unable to find a steep enough discount anywhere. She checks her bank account in the mornings, her student loan balance and credit card bills in the evenings. She calls her mom on Sundays and tries to sound cheerful, like a successful young graduate. If she loses the bet, she'll have to cancel her OB/GYN appointment. She suspects, if she wins, Alexis will claim the bet was a joke.

A half dozen nights in October, Lorene jolts awake from dreams in which a smoky white thing crouches beside her bed. When she swipes on her phone flashlight, nothing's in the room. It happens at 4:37 a.m. Then 4:19, 3:59, 3:31, 3:06, 2:52, her inner clock ticking backward in time. She hunts for Saint Sebastian on his broken chain. She finds him on the nightstand, on the dresser by her earring tree, on the shelf in her closet, tucked into her left Ghost. She can't remember moving him.

Marathon morning, when her alarm yanks her to consciousness, her panties are soaked. Her period's early. It should be okay, though. The agony arrives hours after the blood, like a too-cool cousin at a family reunion. She plans to have finished the race by then.

She changes into her period underwear and tiptoes to the bathroom with the bloody panties squished in her fist. The light, snapping on over the spotted mirror, assaults her eyes. Blinking, she tosses her panties into the sink and retrieves the cup from her toiletry bag. As usual, insertion aches and then feels like nothing.

While Lorene rinses out the soiled panties, a pale shadow invades her periphery. She jerks around and stares at the bathroom window: peeling frame, hand-crank opener, thready duct tape sticking the screen in place, her blurry reflection in the black glass.

That's all it is. Her own reflection.

FOR THE FIRST EIGHTEEN MILES, Lorene's clockwork. She knocks back a paper cup at every water stop, slurps GU gels at thirty-minute intervals, and dogs a petite Black woman in purple spandex running seven-and-a-half-minute miles.

Lorene turns to cement around mile nineteen. When she chokes down two gels in a row, hoping for energy, they heave back up her esophagus. She slows, swallowing and massaging her sweaty throat till the puke threat passes.

Her Garmin says she's barely hitting a ten-minute/mile pace. She tries to speed up. Can't. Her legs feel jointless and bottom-heavy, Gumby-esque. She tastes humiliation, pictures Alexis's Cheshire smirk floating ahead of her. She wants to quit. She palms her compression shorts' back pocket, where she zipped Saint Sebastian before she left the house, and shambles on.

Past the twenty-one-mile marker, a pallor blanches her vision.

The course map unfolds in her mind: O'Reilly Chapel Road intersects the route near here. Every third street in this town is Chapel Hill, Woods, Drive, or Tower, but in this case, it could signal a nearby cemetery.

Or maybe Iffy, not dead, needs no hallowed ground to manifest.

Features surface in Iffy's smoky face. She grins, teeth roots clear through transparent gums, and snatches at Lorene's shoulder.

Lorene strangles a scream and takes off.

Terror hurls her through miles twenty-two, twenty-three, twenty-four. Iffy lopes a step behind. Beyond the strain in Lorene's thighs, the tearing in her lungs, she intuits menstrual pain approaching too soon, like thunderclouds piling on the horizon. She can't stop. She has to outrun it.

Beyond the twenty-five-mile marker, near the intersection with Massey Chapel Road, pain knifes her between navel and crotch and swivels around like it's locating something. Lorene buckles at the waist, clutching her stomach. An older woman with a true endurance athlete's blank, inward-focused eyes swerves around her and bounds ahead, ropy calves twitching. At the same time, Iffy leaps and throws out a hand. A nail slices Lorene's neck.

Lorene staggers forward. Iffy vanishes.

Hot liquid trickles down Lorene's thigh. She assumes she pissed herself, but when she swipes at the wet patch on her black shorts, her fingers come away red. The cup's vacuum seal must have broken inside her.

The last water stop appears. Behind volunteers offering paper cups stand three yellow port-a-potties. She veers around a hairy runner slopping water into his beard and careens into the closest one.

She latches the door, peels down her shorts, and collapses onto the seat. Urinal cake and runner's diarrhea scent the cramped space. Her hands shake so hard she has trouble gripping the cup, but she tugs it out, dumps it, reinserts, twists to seal.

She wipes her fingers and thighs with toilet paper. When they're sort of clean, she palms her wet neck and examines her hand. Red again. Not the black-adjacent carmine of menstrual blood but a bright red like cherry candy. Iffy scratched her deep. It hurts. It's real.

Lorene checks her watch. If she runs the final mile in eight minutes, she'll qualify for Boston.

Her abdomen is swollen and hot, an infected wound. But she pushes up from the seat—more germs—and stands. Rolls up her shorts. Fumbles at her back for the pocket zip. Grabs Saint Sebastian. Some impulse tells her to cast him into the toilet's fetid mouth.

She tightens her fist around him and reaches for the latch. Maybe Iffy—forever eighteen, streaming a ribbon from her thigh—will be waiting outside. Maybe she'll meet Lorene's eye and smile, baring see-through gums and opaque teeth. Maybe she'll slash a fingernail across Lorene's throat.

Maybe she'll chase Lorene across the finish line.

Come back, Lorene prays. *I need you behind me. I need you.*

She opens the door. ◆

KRISTA JAHNKE
PRIMO

THE DEVIANT ACTS started small. On an otherwise forgettable Wednesday, Charlotte stopped typing an email and swiped the stapler from her cubicle neighbor's desk. George was on vacation (again), and it was his rather rude client she'd been emailing. Charlotte walked with the stapler to the kitchenette and eyed the freezer. She placed the stapler inside. The following Monday, when no colleague had mentioned the stapler sitting in the break room freezer, she went back and threw it in the trash. It landed with a satisfying *thunk,* and Charlotte warmed her hands, chilly from the brief handling, under hot water.

The prevailing sense of mischief she felt reminded her of being a girl, playing pranks on her brothers. A warmth bloomed in her belly, an inner fire, which she welcomed.

George returned from vacation two days later with a forehead sunburn and crass stories about the tiki bar at the hotel pool.

"This one chick's bikini," he told Kenny, a kangaroo-shaped man who hovered in their space like a conjured spirit. "Two little strings, triangles, barely anything." George drew triangles over the lumpy chest compressed under his dress shirt.

"You got a picture?"

"Not one I can share here anyway." They laughed.

Charlotte—compact with a pile of curly hair—reached into a drawer and retrieved a few pieces of blank white paper. She cleared her throat. "Does anyone have a stapler I can borrow?"

Like a startled baby, Kenny flailed at the sound of her voice and whipped around. "Oh. Hey, Charlotte," he said. George fumbled around, moving errant documents and file folders. He shuffled a newspaper from one stack to another. His crispy brow rumpled into furrowed creases.

"Not sure where my stapler went. You seen it?"

"Nope," Charlotte said brightly. "Weird. You know what, never mind. I don't need one now."

The image of George unraveling his desk gave her life for a few days. Messing with an inconsequential man who once was late to work because he'd drunkenly locked himself in his garage was beneath her, but behaving badly in these tiny, inconsequential ways felt like a newfound joy.

She tried other feats of sabotage. She grabbed a document fresh off the printer and sailed it into the recycling bin. She emptied a colleague's cup of pens into her purse on the way out the door. A coworker's notebook fell under her chair, and she kicked it under the nearby file cabinet, where the woman struggled to find it.

On her commute, she popped her gum and tried to care about the labels that applied to her. She was a mean-spirited bitch! A basketcase! A crazy wackjob! She found she couldn't make herself care.

Two weeks after the stapler incident, she stalled at her desk while the rest of the team gathered in the boardroom. Larry, who frequently told her to smile, had left his coffee on his desk, still steaming. She palmed it and walked to her boss, Leann's office. Charlotte dumped Larry's coffee in Leann's seat and left the mug beside her rolling chair. The coffee saturated the plump cushion of the seat, spreading out like an ink blot.

As she entered the boardroom moments later, everyone stared out the large windows along the back. The view overlooked a small pond. Someone had spotted a fox skirting between the tall grasses, its red fur unmistakable.

"What was that song? 'What Does the Fox Say?' Remember?" cackled Dee Dee. She sang a few bars, her voice shrill. Finally, the excitement died down, and people took their seats. Rather than sit at the long conference table that anchored the room, Charlotte sat to the side in a chair along the wall. Leanne had made clear months ago that this was where Charlotte belonged. She'd waited until after a meeting during which everyone had sat, in Charlotte's opinion, comfortably snug around the table. But Leann touched her arm and explained how she'd appreciate it if Charlotte would take a spot along the wall. Nothing personal, but she needed to ensure the account reps were not crowded.

It was the "nothing personal" that got to her. She repeated those words at night as she paced the family room of her small bungalow. *Nothing personal, nothing personal.*

When she started reporting to Leann, she'd thought they could be the kind of boss-subordinate pair who might get a drink together after work. It hadn't worked out that way. Leann didn't share anecdotes about her weekends. She offered no hints at her hobbies, nothing that could bond them. She kept her cards close to her vest.

It did feel personal. Charlotte sensed there was something off about herself. She was like an odorless vapor passing through every space unnoticed. People didn't make eye contact with her. She rarely received invites out. It was like she'd turned forty and disappeared. That's where this, some might say unhinged, desire to commit random acts of chaos, to fuck with people, settled on her like a cloudy spritz of drugstore perfume, impossible to wash off.

After the meeting, back at their desks, Larry's phone rang. He hustled to Leann's office and returned fifteen minutes later, his face a cross between confused and angry, like two emojis glitching. He held the mug and glowered at the room. "Who the *fuck* took my coffee and threw it all over Leann's office—because it sure as hell wasn't me!" he yelled. "There are cameras, you know! You will get caught!" He banged the coffee cup on his desk.

Charlotte stared at her keyboard and tried to calm the little hairs on the back of her neck. Cameras hadn't occurred to her.

Leann brought the incident to the next staff meeting. "Someone poured coffee all over my chair. I would like the person who did it to come forward."

She explained that the camera in the hallway wasn't working at the time. She explained that she needs everyone's help to restore the culture of respect in their workplace.

After a lengthy pause, George stood and turned, hands on his hips. "Can I share something? Maybe related, maybe not. But someone threw my stapler in the garbage." A murmur bloomed. "Yeah, I couldn't find it one day, and Kenny told me he saw it in the freezer of all places—and then a day later, in the garbage."

Across the room, Kenny nodded solemnly. "I left it in the garbage because I thought it was busted. But it was George's!"

Charlotte stifled a laugh. The fire in her belly popped like someone had laid a fresh, dry log on it.

She waited one week to strike again. Charlotte went to the office before 7 a.m. on a Friday in early summer; the sky brightened to a faint and delicate blue. Inside, it was still and serene. She took the stairs to Leann's dark office. She shut the door behind her. An abstract painting hung over Leann's desk. Its deep oranges and reds stood out against the bone-colored walls. It had never added up that it was Leann's. It didn't seem to be her taste. Leann wore elegant suits, hair in a bob, and tasteful modest jewelry. Even on casual Fridays, Leann didn't wear jeans. She ate sensible lunches—salads with dressing on the side, brothy soups. She criticized their memos, marking them with a red pen, and failed to laugh at the jokes before meetings started. This exuberant, emotive, bold painting defied Leann's cold, sterile brand. It was out of place. So she'd take it.

Charlotte pulled a white sheet from her work bag. She yanked the painting from the wall and covered it, bundling the sheet a few times around the canvas, cocooning it like a baby. It was light in her arms as she walked back into the hallway, down the deserted stairway, and to the parking lot. One car sat near hers with brake lights beaming. It hadn't been there when she went in. Someone was in the driver's seat. Charlotte hustled past and glanced with a side-eye through the window to see Dee Dee applying mascara in her rearview. Dee Dee didn't look her way, and Charlotte hurried, hoping her footsteps were quiet enough. She arrived at her car, opened the trunk, placed the smuggled artwork inside, and closed the door with a muffled boom. As she started toward the building, Dee Dee popped out of her car.

"Charlotte, morning," Dee Dee's eyes blinked behind her darkened lashes. "You're traveling light today, eh?"

"Traveling light?"

"No work bag?"

She'd left it in Leann's office. Damn it. Her face warmed.

"Oh, I left my bag here last night. That's why I came in today anyway."

Dee Dee's gaze turned to the pond area. "Hey, want to see if we can find that fox?"

"The fox?"

"Yeah, by the pond. He's there somewhere."

"I don't think foxes usually hang out in the open."

Dee Dee shifted her bag and looked away from Charlotte. "I know, it's probably silly. I just would love to see him, you know?"

Charlotte didn't want to traipse around, invading the fox's space. What if she was territorial, with a den full of pups? "I think it's a she, the fox," Charlotte said as they walked in. "For what it's worth."

While Dee Dee went to get coffee, Charlotte hurried to grab her bag from Leann's office. She was back a minute later, and Dee Dee was at her desk, sipping away. She said nothing as Charlotte walked past her with her bag at her side.

That weekend, she listed more productive ways to spend her time. She could take up crocheting, propagate a houseplant, or even get a pet, maybe a songbird. She could schedule a vacation somewhere far away, Morocco or Singapore. She could make new friends. She could get involved in politics and go door to door for some good cause. (She crossed that one off quickly.) She could buy a rowing machine or learn how to perfect a cat eye. She could plant a raised garden bed and grow her cucumbers.

Final bullet: she could talk to Leann, confess her crime, and explain herself. She could ask Leann how to be taken seriously.

Once done, she re-read the list, crumpled it into a ball, and threw it away.

The retribution for her prank came on Monday. At the staff meeting that afternoon, Leann huddled with the company president, Eugene, as the staff assembled. He nodded compassionately to Leann, his lips thin and grim, and placed his hand on her arm, almost tenderly, as a father might. Leann looked like she'd been crying, her shoulders hunched and her skin splotchy. The meeting began, and fifteen minutes in, after updates about the still-not-working cameras, Leann stepped to the podium. Her breath sounded ragged and hot. She unfolded a piece of paper and read.

"This morning, I came in, and my painting was gone. I've looked all over. It's not on my desk, not on the floor. I've asked the custodial staff, and no one knows where it might be. I can only assume this is another act of theft or vandalism." She paused, tears wetting her eyes. "I have shared this with HR and Eugene. We all deserve to work in a place where our things are respected. So please, if you know anything about this, say something."

She folded the paper and stepped away from the podium before she changed her mind and returned. After a pause, she spoke in a softer voice. "That artwork is very meaningful to me. Please, if you took it, return it."

That evening, Charlotte carried the painting inside and unwrapped it on her couch. There were few clues to its deeper meaning. The colors swirled together in broad strokes without forming recognizable shapes. Charlotte flicked on every light and examined more closely. Ah! There—scraps of sheet music were arranged in the clearings between the colors. The vivid colors mostly obscured them. One such snippet included what looked like a song title—"Primo." Charlotte Googled it, but without a composer or any other reference, the search yielded no promising results. She picked up the painting and moved to her kitchen, where the light was better. She brushed against something taped to the back as she grasped it. She flipped the painting over to discover a white envelope. From inside it, she pulled out a piece of paper. It read:

For Primo.

It was signed, "Your darling, Andre."

Charlotte examined again and found a stamp, some kind of authentication, with a date and address behind the envelope. It belonged to a gallery a few miles away.

THAT SATURDAY, a gaggle of kids wearing the same red shirt filled the gallery, there on some field trip. She passed through the scrawl, noting how ill-behaved and loud the kids were, and located a woman clad all in black save for a white geometric necklace of interlocking squares draped down the front of her chest.

"Excuse me," Charlotte said. "I'm interested in the work of an artist, Andre something. I'm sorry, I can't recall his last name. Ring a bell? I think I saw his work here before."

The woman typed on her keyboard without looking up and replied, "Andre Douglas. He's local. Did a show here a couple of years ago."

She reached out to hand Charlotte his card. It included his website and social media handles. Outside, Charlotte found a bench and examined Andre Douglas' Instagram page. It consisted of posts about upcoming shows, shots of his work, and a few selfies. Despite his fading hairline, he was handsome with soulful brown eyes and a scruffy beard. She flicked her thumb, refreshing the feed, hoping to find a photo of the artwork called Primo.

Then she came to the baby picture. Posted almost two years ago, it showed a baby sleeping, wrapped in a blanket. Brand new, tiny, its scrunched face a pale pink. The caption said, "Rest in peace, my Primo."

Her chest had opened up to the morning air, and a chill rushed in. The kids' gleeful yells seeped through the door, their voices muffled but effervescent and jagged with joy. So goddamned loud and happy they were! She scrolled to see if there were more photos of the boy but found none. Nothing. No other sign of him, no reference to his existence until the post announcing his death.

Over the next few days, she returned to the photo. She searched the boy's small face for signs of Leann's. She opened Leann's photo on the company website and compared their faces. Since Leann became her boss the previous year, they'd never talked about kids, and Charlotte had assumed she didn't have any. She didn't display any photos in her office. She'd never mentioned a partner. If she were to write a list of what she knew about Leann, it would be quite short.

One night, emboldened by three glasses of wine, Charlotte created a new Instagram profile. She posted art photos to it, photos she right-clicked and saved from various websites. She did this every day for weeks. She followed artists and collectors and dotted her posts with popular art hashtags. A new persona, that of an avid art connoisseur, formed post by post. Each evening, she made a new post and visited Primo's picture, mesmerized by the tiny folds of his eyelids and the tint of his pink skin.

At work, the investigation for the art thief stalled; no new messages from HR arrived in her inbox. One day, while in the supply room, she spotted the extra staplers and brought one to George. She handed it over with a shrug, explaining that she knew he'd lost his. During meetings, Charlotte sank into her seat against the wall, where Leann had relegated her. She watched Leann closely, detecting a new weariness in her posture.

The fox appeared again a month later, slipping between the cattails with something dangling in its teeth. It moved with grace and urgency, and as they all crowded by the window to see it, Charlotte sensed again that it was a mother returning to feed her cubs a mutilated mouse or an unlucky groundhog. What choice did it have but to seek blood? It could choose, she supposed, to respect and honor the life of the other animals in its habitat, to eat berries or other foliage, but that would be unnatural—it would mean a slow death.

After a month, Charlotte sent Andre a message from her fake account.

I purchased a painting of yours at an estate sale. I would love to know more about it. Could I send a photo?

He responded two days later.

Certainly, fire away.

Charlotte sent a photo of the painting leaning against the fence outside. He responded within fifteen minutes.

Where did you say you purchased it?

Charlotte went for a walk to think about her reply, then wrote: *An estate sale. I can't recall the address, it was a few weeks back.*

His reply showed up a minute later.

Interesting. I'd like to buy it back from you. Can we meet?

They arranged for the following Saturday. A café in town, a little French place, with a resident bulldog named Pierre. That Friday, Charlotte sought out Leann before she left for the day. She hovered in her office doorway until Leann asked her to come in.

"Yes, Charlotte?" Leann said.

"I wondered, did you ever find your painting?"

Leann's eyebrows creased in surprise.

"No. It never turned up."

"I'm sorry to hear that. You said it was meaningful to you?"

Leann fidgeted with her pen as if deciding what to reveal, twisting it in her fingers. "Yes. Very."

Charlotte waited to see if she would say more. But Leann had turned her body to her computer. A moment passed. Charlotte waited but didn't prod further. A curtain closed.

"Well, I always liked it," Charlotte said. "I'm sure it will turn up."

She closed the door.

On Saturday, Charlotte placed the painting in a large department store bag and drove to the cafe. Andre was scheduled to arrive at 8. At 7:45, she walked in and ordered a latte. While the barista prepared it, she pulled the painting from the bag and propped it on a chair near the front window. She sat a few tables away to wait and opened a book.

A few minutes later, Andre walked toward the door. From outside, he clocked the painting in the window. His pace quickened, and he beelined for it once inside. He picked it up and studied it.

"Excuse me," he said to her. "Did you see who left this here?"

She feigned annoyance, tapping her foot. "What's that?"

"Sorry, I know this is odd, but did you see someone place this painting here?"

"No, sorry. I've been reading."

"No worries," he chuckled. "This is my painting."

"You painted that?" Charlotte hoped she sounded authentic and not as high-pitched as in her head.

"Yes. I was supposed to meet someone here to ... reacquire it."

"I guess they left it for you."

"I suppose so," he said.

"It's a lovely painting," Charlotte said. "Any story behind it?"

His eyes crumbled inward, his lids sinking, his irises tightening into two pinpricks of light.

"It's in honor of my son," he said. "He died very young."

"Oh, dear. I'm so sorry," Charlotte said.

"It has little bits of a song called "Primo" that we used to sing to him in the background. See?"

He brought it close to her and pointed to the music scraps.

"Ah, I see. So his name was Primo?"

"No, that was just what we called him. His name was Lee. A family name."

"Ah. You must be so happy to have it back. It's horrible that someone would steal something so precious from you."

"From my sister. I gave it to her because she's the one who introduced that song, and it just made his little face light up. It disappeared a couple of months ago from her office."

A nephew then. Leann, a doting aunt, and Lee, her namesake nephew.

She thought the fact that it wasn't a mother's grief Leann was wading through would release a layer of guilt. Instead, a shameful feeling fluttered and landed on her like a flock of birds coming to roost all at once. Her arms weighed down. She suddenly worried she might cry.

"Well," Charlotte stood and moved toward the door. "Your sister will be so happy you've got it back, I'm sure."

He smiled at her with an undeserved kindness that arrowed into her chest. "Nice that things work out sometimes." He started toward the exit behind her but stopped. "Wait, how did you know it was stolen?"

Charlotte's hand gripped the handle, and she imagined the door to the parking lot as a portal. Later, after she packed her desk and quit, she imagined what might have happened if she'd stopped then, turned, and revealed her culpability. That would have been the brave thing to do. Instead, she'd opened the door and walked out without answering him.

Andre hadn't mentioned Leann was there, waiting in the car idling right by the door. As she stepped out, she and Leann locked eyes. Leann's face opened into a silent snarl. Her lips moved, and while Charlotte couldn't make out the words, she sensed the accusation. Charlotte gave her a pitiful wave and trotted to her car. Then she drove away.

Charlotte kept the memory of this time of bad deeds locked into a remote part of her memory for the rest of her life. She didn't speak of them. She never mentioned them to the man she eventually married. Sometimes, she sensed a desire to let a fire sparkle low and quiet in her again. It reminded her she was utterly alive, capable of many things, not unlike the fox. Knowing what dwelled in her was at least an honest way to be. ◆

MARK HARRIS

UNFOLDING

The feed also shows
unclaimed belongings, shadows
gone from short to long,
a day moon. One of the dead
is said to be the shooter.

DELAY

My daughter unlocks
my device and a sad song
from this morning begins
to play. It's these short days, late
hours, the suffering earth.

NATALIE HOMER

HARVEST

The pretty book disappoints
and yellow tinges the wild hedges
too early, I think again, year after year.
I've never had candied violets, but they sound nice.
Something nice I *have* had:
your tongue seeking mine.

There's much to worry about losing—
bees   ice   ozone   being desired.
Late August, every day seems like the first day
of something. I test a grape   then a blackberry
from our vines. Both are sour
as they come.

RETURN TRIP

New subdivisions grow where wheat used to
in the town I no longer think of as home.

Here, the tower light flashes its white warning
against a backdrop of storm-purple sky,
and a bird discards a bit of grapevine on the porch.

The orchids are party favors to keep.
Three ice cubes a week
says a note attached, in marker.

My parents have new horses
with names I don't recognize.
Which reminds me   were you the type
to pick out the horse you wanted
while you waited for your turn on the carousel?

I keep checking for the coyote
I saw once
in the patch of West Virginia wildflowers
beside the highway.
Today I realized   I've been looking for him
                     for years now.

Meanwhile, the picture my father sends
matches the image in my dream:
clouds cover the mountain
framed through the cabin's window.

CECY VILLARRUEL

GRIEVING IN TEOCUITATLÁN

My father was silent on the day of the funeral,
speaking only once as he pointed at cacti from the car.
He said as a child he would walk along the dusty road
picking pitayas off the cacti to devour them.

His father told him it was the closest he'd ever get
to eating a heart or kissing a beautiful woman.

After the funeral, Dad pulled over
and parked by a great big cactus.
He pulled off a couple pitayas and gave me one
without saying a word.

KATHERINE CONNER
SNAKE'S TONGUE

ANYTHING CAN TURN UP IN WATER, Iris's father used to say. And things have been turning up for weeks. The river, swollen from spring rain, so high Iris can see it from the window of Gator's Tube and Canoe Rental while she rings up customers. Shimmer of the sun against the water, like the glint of scales off the back of some slow-moving beast.

It brings things back. A woman's high-heeled shoe, an old cell phone, a baseball glove, water-rotted and slick with slime, a boy's initials blurred into the leather. All of it carried to the riverbank by the sluggish, muddy current. Things nobody wants anymore. Nobody but Iris. She'd taken them home, arranged them on top of her dresser, a display of lost things still damp with river water. The loamy smell of them, as if she brought the river home with her, and she keeps glancing over at the muddy bank, keeps waiting for what will turn up next.

"Stop looking," Ben, her boss, says. He's helping her ring up customers. It's crowded, the first Saturday of unofficial summer, a restlessness in the air, a hum of energy. Group after group of tubers buying sunblock and bug spray and cellophane-wrapped sandwiches. "Ain't going to flood."

But that's not what makes her tense, her nerves strung so tight her skin feels stretched, shiny taut over her knuckles, her ribs, the blades of her collar bone. Like there's a second skin underneath, ready to push its way out. It's something else. Something else her father once said: anything can turn up in water, but anything can disappear too. Like that girl a couple of years back. The one who brought so much trouble with her. Not a sign of her since.

IN THE PURPLE GLOW OF DUSK, after Iris has shut down the register at Gator's, after she has swept the floor and wiped the counter and refilled the coolers with cans of Coke and overpriced bottles of water, she heads out back where the canoe boys spray down all the canoes and tubes at the end of the day. But there's no one there, all of them gone home already. The canoes and tubes locked up in the shed. Even Ben has left, his blue truck gone from the gravel lot. No one checked to see if she was still here. To tell her goodbye, have a nice night, see you tomorrow. No one ever does.

It's later than usual, she realizes, the light fading out behind the trees, branches melting into violet sky, everything blending. Like water. "All this water connected," her father once told her and her sister Daisy. He used to be a ranger at the state park, and he liked to talk about rivers and sloughs and backwaters, how one water became another and another. He had a whole collection of maps of all the rivers in the country. His favorite one, *Mississippi Rivers, Streams, and Lakes*, still hangs, framed, on the wall in the den above his chair. Skinny blue lines of the rivers, like the map's veins, pumping watery blood.

"See," her father said to Daisy and Iris. "I work there." He pointed to a spot on the map. "North of us, before the river forks." He moved his finger down an inch. "See the fork?" His fingertip hovered in the air above the glass. "Right by us, where we live."

Iris squinted at the map. So much water, all those squiggly streams and rivers, like a child's scribble, like the pictures she and her sister used to draw that, later, their mother would stick on the refrigerator. Meaningless scrawl. But sometimes, when no one was around, Iris would stare at the map so long all those lines would blur together, become one glimmering water she could slip down into, so cool, so blue. She would imagine herself emerging from it, shiny and wet, her eyes dark with some secret knowledge.

"*Here.*" He touched the glass this time. Whorl of his fingerprint there, like his own ghostly water, a faint estuary superimposed over the lakes and rivers. "See, girls?"

Daisy shook her head.

"I see it," Iris said, even though she didn't. "I see the fork. Looks like a snake's tongue."

Her father turned to her, his face lit up. His handsome face, dimples showing. "Snake's tongue," he said. "I guess it does."

That was years ago now, before Iris got the job at Gator's, working just below the snake's tongue, on the east side of the river. Before all her drawings on the refrigerator had yellowed and curled up at the corners. Before they were replaced with cut-out coupons and flyers for take-out food and classified ads ripped from the paper. Before the girl went missing at the state park. Before Iris's father was stripped of his ranger's duties, forced to resign. Before her mother started drinking too much, before she left.

After, he didn't talk so much about rivers anymore. He doesn't talk much at all these days, the two of them passing one another silently in the house, Iris on her way to the bathroom, her father shuffling to the kitchen. She'll come home sometimes on a day he's not at work to find him slumped in his chair in the den, the TV blaring some British baking show. "Hey, Dad," she always says, but he rarely replies, rarely looks at her. A grunt, a nod. That's all.

But then, about a month ago, just as the river began to swell, Iris found him standing in front of the map. "Hey, Dad," she said, like always. And this time, he spoke. "Tines," he said, and she had no idea what he meant at first. "Two sides of a snake's tongue. They're like tines." He didn't look at her as he talked, kept staring at the map. "Both tines empty out in the same spot." He pressed his palm against his forehead, as if he had a pain there. Or a sudden thought. "It all ends up in the Gulf."

She wanted to show him the woman's high-heeled shoe she'd just found, tell him it ended up not in the Gulf, but *here*, with her. Wanted to know what he thought of that.

But he'd gone quiet, that flat look he gets, his face slackened, dimples gone, his eyes unfocused. The look he had the day the girl went missing. Same look he had for days and days while the police interrogated him, served him warrants, searched his truck. A look she can't penetrate, like he's gone somewhere else, sunk deep. Sucked into the open mouth of the river, swallowed down so far Iris can't find him even on the map.

A thought scuttles at the corner of her consciousness, shows itself before she can shoo it away: she's not sure she'd want to find him, if she could.

DARK COMING ON FAST NOW, seeping across the sky, and she should go. Should pull her bike from under the porch steps and cycle the two miles back to her father's house. But he's not home now, she knows. Won't be home for hours yet. Working nights as a fry cook at the Waffle House up in Brookhaven. Her mother not there either, gone off with her boyfriend to Florida. Daisy married already and living in Bogalusa. No one waiting on Iris. No one warming supper on the stove. No one worrying about where she is.

So she takes her time, gathers her things—her keys, the bright blue drawstring backpack she carries everywhere, so worn now the nylon is nearly see-through at the bottom. They'd found it on the river. Iris and her father, Daisy, their mother. A long time ago now, Iris and Daisy still in grade school. They'd rented a couple of canoes for an afternoon. When they stopped on a hot stretch of sand for lunch, there was the backpack, balled up in the weeds like some bright nesting bird. Iris snatched it before Daisy could lay claim to it first, showed it to her father.

"Whose is it?" she asked.

He looked at it, shrugged. "Yours."

Hers, this lost thing, and she used to imagine where it came from, how far up the river. How far up the map. She slings the backpack over her arm now, thinks about the missing girl. She thinks about her a lot, another lost thing. Her photo on all those flyers, her thick dark hair, her little upturned nose, her face right up in the camera, a selfie. *Last seen wearing a pink tank top with a red lipstick kiss on the front.*

If Iris herself went missing, no one would remember what she was wearing. Always the same—jean shorts, some washed-out tee shirt. Her backpack the only spot of color, such a bright, cobalt blue. The most memorable thing about her.

But people change when they disappear, become memorable just because they're gone. An air of mystery about a missing person, something alluring. Like the lost things that turn up in the river. Touched by magic, as if the water itself has ascribed some kind of meaning to their existence. Has made them special.

Her eyes burn, and she realizes she's been standing there without blinking, just gazing out over the store's porch at the stretch of road beyond. She pulls the strings of her backpack tight under her arms and goes around back again to check that the shed is locked—the canoe boys are stoned half the time, prone to forget things—and a sound in the distance, up by the riverbank, makes her pause. A sound like a voice, mumbling something low, urgent.

"Hello?" Iris says, and it comes out thin, warbling. The uncertainty of a scared girl. She clears her throat, tries again. "Hello?"

Nothing. No answer, the voice gone now. She stares for a moment at the spot where the trees crowd close over the bank. All she hears is the murmur of slow-moving water, the river's soft, steady breath.

SHE'S PEDALING FAST, playing the voice over and over in her head, trying to piece the sounds together into words. Half a mile from Gator's, something clicks. *Tell*, it sounded like it was saying. *Tell you.* She slows the bike to a stop on the grassy shoulder of the road. Stands there, legs straddling the saddle, fingers clenched tight around the handlebars.

Tell you. That could've been it. *I want to tell you.*

Crickets trill, loud in the dark. A frog moans, low and throaty, from the ditch along the road's shoulder. If she shined a light there, red eyes would glow back at her, alligators silent in the shallow water. Watching her with their ancient, half-hooded eyes, as if waiting for her to decide: does she want to know? She's not sure, but she jerks the handlebars around and pedals back.

IRIS'S FATHER didn't go back. When the girl went missing, he didn't go back for her. It was one of the questions asked over and over. *Why didn't he go back?* The papers, the reporters, the commenters online all wanted to know.

He saw the girl out there alone, out there in the state park, at the edge of the river, just wandering around barefoot. He talked to her, he said, convinced her to get in his truck. The official ranger's truck, white with *U.S. Park Ranger* on the side. He was proud of that truck. Proud of that job, so handsome in his uniform, his Stetson hat always set at just the right angle atop his head. A striking figure, picturesque, like something out of a movie, and park-goers would stop to take his picture, would pose alongside him. His firm, set jaw, his blue eyes. His dimples.

Later, some of those very photos would show up on the front page of local newspapers and websites. *Ranger Lane Sullivan Named 'Person of Interest' in Teen's Disappearance* and *State Park Ranger Last Person to See Missing Girl Alive.* Iris read them all, each and every story she could find. And all of them asked the same question. Why didn't he go back? If the girl had done what he claimed, had thrown the truck door open and ran—why didn't he go back to find her?

He never had an answer. All he ever said was he watched her walk west, away from the river, back toward the park's Visitor's Center and the parking lot. She walked west, he said, and that was all he knew.

But sometimes Iris imagines her, not west, but south, following the river down to its fork, to the place where all the squiggly lines overlapped. Swallowed up in it, that scribble. A part of it now, her skinny legs another tiny stream, her dark hair a tangled pond, her arms over her head in a V, a fork. A snake's tongue.

NEARLY FULL DARK by the time she's back at Gator's. A sliver-moon hanging low in the sky. She leans her bike against the porch, pulls her phone from her backpack, turns on its flashlight. She's sweating, her tee shirt stuck to her chest, her thighs tense from pedaling so fast and hard. Her damp fingers leave imprints on her phone's screen, a fingertip eddy, a streaky rivulet. She makes her way through the parking lot, feet crunching over the gravel, then rounds the side of the gift shop, back by the shed.

Everything so dark, so strange in the white glow of her phone's flashlight. Like a place she's never been, dream-like, blurred at the edges. And the river, black against the indigo sky. Mumbling at her, words whispered as if right into her ear. A sound that follows her every night, long after she has gone home. Her father's house is too far from the river to hear it, but Iris hears it anyway, the rise and fall of its hushed breath, lulling her to sleep like a lover curled up next to her on her little twin bed, sighing against her cheek. She steps closer to the water, her sneakers sinking into the mud. Tilts her head, as if to catch what it's saying, but it's never clear. A babbling she can never make out.

Not like the voice earlier. *I want to tell you.*

She turns, and the light sweeps across something crumpled on the bank, right beneath the spindly pine branches where she'd heard the voice. Heat slithers up from the pit of her stomach, coils into a fist inside her chest. A prickle over her scalp, her skin tingling—*stretching*—up the back of her neck. She moves, silent, over the soft bank, the light wavering in her shaking hand until she's close enough to touch it, this dim, shapeless thing. She shines the light down on it—some kind of cloth. She bends, picks it up, clammy, damp, an odor of mildew, age. Something familiar about it, the faded pink color of the cloth, and that coiled heat in her chest knots tighter, tighter, and she drops onto her knees in the sandy dirt, spreads the cloth out. Runs the light over it, up and down and back up again.

Rotted, dirt caked around the neck hole and across the hem. But still, she can tell what it is. A pink tank top with a red lipstick kiss.

SHE BIKES HOME as fast as she can, the tank top wadded up in a ball and stuffed into her backpack, slapping against her back as she pedals. Crickets and cicadas shriek at her from the trees, the only noise on this dead backwoods road but the noise she makes herself, her panting breath, the whir of her tires against the pavement. So alone out here, nothing but the black road cowled in trees, the branches interwoven overhead like laced fingers, cupped palms, holding her in.

Finally, she reaches the house. The driveway empty, her father still gone, of course. He won't be home for hours yet. She throws her bike on the overgrown lawn and rushes up the creaking porch steps, hands fumbling with her keys. She slams the door shut and snaps the bolt, then slips the chain lock in place. Stops, turns back, takes the chain off. Her father will need to get in later.

A shiver runs up her spine as she thinks of him. Of what else might turn up in the river.

In her room, the door shut, she glances at her dresser where the other things, the high-heeled shoe, the phone, the baseball glove, sit side by side. She pulls the tank top out of her backpack. Shakes it gently, and dried mud flakes off, spatters across the worn green carpet. She holds it up with the tips of her fingers, so small. The girl was small. Only sixteen, skinny, her gangly legs pulled up to her chest in one of the photos on her Facebook page. Iris has scrolled through them all. Meredith Beverly, her dark hair, her coltish young body. Puckering her lips in selfie after selfie, another duck-faced girl usually crammed up beside her, cheek to cheek. *Cheer camp with my girls!* And *#besties* and one captioned with a series of heart emojis.

Just another teenage girl. But *You were a shining light,* someone has written beneath the photo. *The world is dark without you.* Special, now that she's gone.

She'd be eighteen now, the girl. Taller, maybe, than the five foot three inches she was when she disappeared. Her face older, full baby cheeks thinner, planes of her cheekbones showing. Another Meredith, the special one, slowly emerging, unsheathing herself. Like when Daisy used to wear too-tight Lycra tops and Iris had to help her peel them off, the moist kiss of spandex pulling away from skin.

What would she say, Daisy, if she knew what Iris found? She gazes at the empty twin bed against the opposite wall. Daisy's old bed, until she moved out. Daisy with the same small brown eyes as Iris, same round face and limp, brown hair. Neither of them inherited their father's good looks, his blue eyes, his striking chin. But sometimes, when Iris smiles just so, a half-smile bunched to one corner of her mouth, a hint of a dimple appears on her left cheek. A dimple like his.

I told you, Daisy might say. But what else? Would she say what neither of them could bring themselves to say out loud before? Would she say,

What if he did it? What if he killed her? Our father.

Their father, who taught them about rivers. Who made pallets on the floor in front of the TV when they were small so they could pile up together and watch cartoons. Who made them grilled peanut butter sandwiches with burnt brown crusts, who took care of them when their mother drank too much wine and fell asleep in the afternoons. Their father who liked the attention from their friends when they got a little older. Who liked it maybe too much, how Daisy's best friend Erin, a pretty blonde, would giggle at all his corny jokes.

Whenever Iris had a sleepover, her girlfriends would say he looked more like a movie-star version of a park ranger than a real one. But that was before—before that handsome face made the front page of all the local papers, before the websites got a hold of the story and ran his photo. Before her girlfriends began to avoid her, to ignore her calls and texts. Before Daisy moved out, before her mother left, before Iris was alone. Alone with him, her father.

"DO YOU THINK everything ends up in the same place?" Later that night, on the phone with Daisy. Iris sits cross-legged on her bed, the tank top folded on her knees. The other things, too, the lost things she'd taken from the riverbank, laid out on the foot of the bed side by side. The high-heeled shoe, a plain black pump, the leather peeling from the heel, and the baseball glove with the initials so swollen Iris can't make them out, and the old cell phone, a Nokia flip phone, its screen cracked.

Daisy sighs into her ear. "What are you talking about?" She's distracted, Iris can tell. Probably watching some program on TV with her husband. It's the first time they've actually talked—other than a few texts now and then—in at least a month.

"Just something Dad said."

"When? Recently?" Daisy hasn't spoken to their father in years. Even before the girl went missing, she'd stopped speaking to him. Stopped coming home most nights, sleeping at her boyfriend's house instead of in the room with Iris. This was just after her friend Erin quit coming over so abruptly. Something happened, and Daisy grew sullen and quiet, her eyes always slit sidewise, suspicious. As soon as she turned eighteen, she left to live with her boyfriend's family. And then they married, and she moved away.

"Look," Daisy says, "I wouldn't listen to anything he says."

"He doesn't say much."

"Look." Her voice sharper. "You should get out. I told you and told you. That house is depressing. You need to go."

"Go *where*?" A jolt of anger runs through her. As if she has any place to go. As if it's that easy.

"Anywhere! Just leave. I did." Another pause, then, as if she's forcing herself to say it, her voice lower, hesitant. "You can come here for a while. I mean, we don't have a lot of room. You'd have to sleep on the couch, and Eric gets up really early for work." She trails off. It's not a real invitation, Iris knows.

"I'll think about it," Iris says, even though she won't. She touches the tank top gently. Clammy damp beneath her fingers. "Daisy," she says before she can lose her nerve. "What happened with Erin?"

A pause so long it becomes more than a pause, a silence that stretches itself thin as one of the map's veins, threading its way to the Gulf.

Then, finally, "I don't know," Daisy says. "She never told me. I saw him take her to the garage to show her his maps. And when they came back, Erin was weird. Asked to go home, said her stomach hurt." Daisy's voice high and wavery, like she's trying not to cry. "And then she just stopped talking to me," she says. "She never talked to me again."

"Did he do something?" Iris is whispering now, even though she's alone, even though her father won't be home for hours. "Did he do something to her?"

"I asked him once."

"What?" Iris sits up, her pulse beating loud in her ears.

"I asked him if he did something to that missing girl. The first thing I'd said to him in a long time."

"You weren't even here then." Iris presses the phone hard to her ear, as if to drown out the rapid beat of her heart. *I want to tell you.*

"I called him. And I asked him point blank. Did you do something to her?"

"What'd he say?"

"The same thing he'd been saying. He said she walked west, and that was all he knew." A rustling sound, Daisy's voice muffled, and Iris imagines her, the phone tucked between her shoulder and her ear. "He said if she'd ended up in the river, something would've turned up by now."

Iris doesn't tell her something has.

"But then," Daisy says, "he said something weird. He said she's probably in the sea. He said everything ends up in the sea."

"The Gulf," Iris says.

"Whatever it is. It didn't make any sense. Like he'd lost his fucking mind."

It does make sense, though. If Daisy had listened to him when they were kids, she would understand. If she'd paid attention when he explained about water. How it's all connected, how one river turns into another and another until it all dumps out into the Gulf. And from the Gulf to the Atlantic. So much water, and Iris closes her eyes, sees it, a vast stretch of blue, waves like glistening scales. Winking in the sun. Beckoning.

HE COMES HOME just past 4:00 AM. Iris is curled on her side in her bed, the room shadowy dark, weak yellow light from the hall slipping through the cracks of the door. She hardly slept, a fitful half-sleep. Aware, even as she slept, of her mattress sagging at the foot of the bed where the boards had collapsed underneath. Aware of the *tick, tick* of the ceiling fan and the stutter of the air conditioner kicking on and the constant lilt of the crickets outside her window.

Aware too of the whisper of the river, stuck in her head, words she can almost make out in the strained quiet. And she lies there, listening, absorbing the quiet, as if drinking it down like a glass of tepid water, the quiet pooling in her stomach until she's water-logged, heavy. Bloated with silence.

And then the click of the lock on the front door, so distinct, like a finger snapping right in her ear. The creak of the door swinging inward, her father's heavy step on the old wood floor. She could jump up from her bed, grab the tank top from the drawer where she stashed it, confront him. It came down the river, she could say. It came from the snake's tongue. You said she went west, but her shirt went south.

It doesn't prove anything, she knows. He could have seen her walk toward the parking lot, just as he said, and she could have circled back after he left. There's no way of knowing. But still, she'd like to see his face, watch him as she slowly unrolls the tank top in her hands and holds it up. Because maybe he'd finally look at her, *see* her. Maybe she'd finally have the nerve to ask him about the times he lingered too long in her bedroom when she had friends over, dimpling his cheeks, laughing and flinging himself beside them on the floor. Maybe she'd ask why he makes things disappear. Erin, Daisy, her mother. Meredith Beverly.

SHE STARES AT THE MAP in the pre-dawn quiet. It's dark in the den, and she presses her face closer, closer until her reflection in the glass looms back at her, gray and ghostly. She reaches out, suddenly, and knocks the frame from the wall. The glass shatters against the floor, loud as a shriek in the dead quiet, and she freezes, that same tight, stretched feeling along the back of her neck, like something pushing its way out. She waits for the creak of her father's door opening, for the thud of his footsteps. But there's nothing.

She picks her way around the broken glass, creeps down the hall to his bedroom door. Stands there, listens. Ragged noise of his breath, rise and fall, the sound of his sleep. As if she's made no noise at all, and she wants to pound on his door with her fists, to scream at him. But, somehow, she knows it won't matter. He won't hear, or he will and he'll open the door and just stand there with his face gone slack, sunk down into himself.

Either way, they'll end up in the same place. Same place they are now, a place without sound or dimension, like a paper cut-out of a house with two stick figures at either corner. Flat and lifeless as the scribbled drawings that once hung on the refrigerator.

She turns and tiptoes back to the den. Crouches, lifts the frame with her fingertips, shakes the broken glass off. Slowly, carefully, she pulls the map from the back of the frame's matting. So much thinner, frailer, than she imagined. The corners yellowed, smell of must and old books.

She carries it to her room, lays it flat on the floor, smooths it with her fingers. The paper crinkles under her palms, a whisper of sound, like the river's breath. She finds the place where her father used to work, the state park. A splotch of green and blue. Trails her finger south, down to where the snake's tongue should be, and still she doesn't see it. Can't make it out among all the other faint lines and colors. She closes her eyes, opens her eyes. She stares at it and stares at it, lets her eyes glaze over, tries to make it become one water, to make it all connect like it used to do when she was a child. But it's still just meaningless scrawl.

She folds the map into a small square, tucks it into her backpack. Dresses in her work clothes—her jean shorts, her sneakers. Starts to pull her Gator's shirt over her head—washed-out gray with a green cartoon alligator on the back—and pauses, tosses it aside. She stands there in her bra and places the lost things from the river into her backpack, one by one. The shoe, the glove, the phone.

The tank top last, but she doesn't put it with the others. She inches her fingers under the hem, shimmies it over her head and shoulders. Moist cloth gritty against her skin, too tight, and she sucks in a breath, tugs it down gently to keep it from ripping. The arm holes cut into her flesh, and a strip of her bare white stomach shows above her shorts. But she feels her, the girl. Imagines she smells her under the mildew smell of rotted cloth—a girl smell of coconut suntan lotion, the musky odor of sweat and skin.

She stares at herself for a moment in the mirror above her dresser, stares at the tank top strained tight over her breasts, still crusted with mud. The red lipstick kiss so faded it's almost not there. She traces her fingertip along the curve of the upper lip, up and down the cupid's bow. A mouth forever puckered in silence.

DAWN COMING UP over the empty road, trees silhouetted against the plum sky. All those limbs overhead, cupping her in, and she pedals fast beneath them toward the pink glow of the sunrise. Higher and higher the sunlight spreads, like glistening water thrown up over her head, and it's nearly full light by the time she reaches Gator's.

No one here yet. They don't open for another two hours. She stows her bike, like always, on its side under the porch. Walks through the empty gravel lot around to the back by the riverbank. Sound of the river, sighing at her before it comes into view, and then there, all at once, as she slips through the mud. Softer in the faint light, a mist coming off it, a gauzy veil.

SHE SLIDES HER BACKPACK off her shoulders, opens it, pulls out the map. Unfolds it, gazes down at all those wavery, senseless lines. Looks up, out at the foggy stretch of river that runs on and on and disappears among the tangled tree limbs. The humid breath of the water envelops her, makes her sweat. Her skin prickles beneath the tank top, the fabric so tight she can't suck in a deep breath, she can't *breathe,* and she drops the map, yanks the hem, threads popping as she pulls it up over her shoulders. She throws it behind her on the bank. Stands there in her bra, chest heaving.

Stands there and listens. To the mutter of the river, the hiss of water forever moving, moving toward the place where everything ends up. *I want to tell you.* And she wants to know.

She bends, grabs the map, holds it up eye-level, and all at once, from among the tangled blue and green, there it is. The fork. Right there, where it must have always been, a V, a flickering snake's tongue. She presses the spot with her finger, and the paper shivers under her fingertip. That stretched, tight feeling again, along the back of her neck, her spine thrumming like a plucked chord.

She steps along the bank, north toward the snake's tongue. Each step lighter and lighter, as if she's shedding herself as she walks. As if she could look back and see her own skin, piled like the pink tank top on the bank. As if whatever's underneath is emerging at last, bit by slinking bit. ◆

JON DAVIS

THE GATHERING

Tipsy though we were, we parked the rental
on the breezy bluff. Gray stones and sheep,
a clatter of waves and wind, three poets
chattering about Shakespeare's sonnets.
Then a scuffle of feet on the stone path,
and Seamus, ten years gone, white shock of hair,
reading by the fire, charming the women
who crowded the bar. Celebrating, we were,
but no one knew quite what—
this passage through air, through rooms
and airports, the fragility of it, the brevity.
We did not know how isolated we'd been.
We'd come out from our homes surprised
to find ourselves unmasked, our bodies
blinged with light and song, the living
and the dead equally at home here.
Here on the Irish coast above the breakers.
There was far to fall and fast. Such was life:
A calling, a fatal falling, but the talk was good.
Books and whiskey, the breath to say
whatever kind or unkind thing—jest
or gesture, some grand theory of everything.
Mostly I recall how we leaned and spoke
like we meant it. And we did, though
we were ephemeral as the terns that scissored
the blustery sky above us, or more so,
there on that improbable bluff. Not even real,
just dream people in our white shirts, wild
somehow about the way words fit together
like fieldstone in a wall. The cobbled wall
that, someone said, would last another

thousand years. "A marvel," Seamus said.
"One of many." And a sadness palled us then.
For we were dying. Or already dead. When finally
someone thought to stir it, the fire ring was cold.

FROM THE PUBLISHER

The price one pays for pursuing any profession or calling is an intimate knowledge of its ugly side. —James Baldwin

OUR MAGAZINE is for the extraordinaries and the visionaries, the eccentrics with integrity. This is why *Raleigh Review* does not ask for donations.

I've never told anyone this story though in the early days of our *Raleigh Review* Writers' Studio in the Five Points neighborhood, I came in a little late one day and our intern at that time met me at the door to say there was someone there waiting to speak to me. The man had a batch of printed poems and his checkbook on the table. He identified himself as the heir to one of the oldest businesses in Raleigh and he told me he wanted his poems published in our magazine, and that he'd pay whatever we asked. I immediately told him we do not operate like this and to read the guidelines on our website. After I turned down his offer to pay us, he asked me to look at his poems anyway so I took a quick look and gave him some pointers and free advice. I did notice the gentleman's poems published in another magazine about a year or so later.

At *Raleigh Review,* we enjoy capturing the stories of lived human experiences. Our ethics are uncompromised, our integrity is intact. As a 501(c)(3) nonprofit organization, *Raleigh Review* has achieved a platinum transparency score via Guidestar's Candid rating system. Rather than placing an emphasis on one time donations, we invite our supporters to subscribe to our magazine, and we hope you will continue doing so. ◆

Rob Greene, publisher

PS: This note is dedicated to our very first subscriber, my Grandmother Barbara Hubbard Greene (1927-2024), who together with my Grandfather Jack E. Greene took me in on numerous occasions when I needed them most. Outside of experiencing this loss, I am very thankful to our talented team with *Raleigh Review* for the opportunity to heal my heart and mind.

contributors

ERIN JONES BENNETT holds an MFA in poetry from the University of Florida. She currently resides in San Antonio, Texas, and works in Student Accessibility Services at Trinity University. Her poems have appeared in *Pleiades, Fourteen Hills, Passages North, Muzzle Magazine,* and elsewhere.

ANDREEA BOBOC grew up in Romania behind the Iron Curtain. She is an associate professor of medieval literature at the University of the Pacific in Stockton, California. "Brahmari's Gift" is her fiction debut.

GEORGE CHOUNDAS is a Cuban- and Greek-American and a former FBI agent. He has published a book of essays (*Until All You See Is Sky,* winner of the EastOver Prize for Nonfiction) and a book of stories (*The Making Sense of Things,* winner of the Ronald Sukenick Innovative Fiction Prize).

KATHERINE CONNER'S collection of stories, *The Hanged Man,* has been selected as a finalist for the 2023 *Iron Horse Literary Review* First Book Prize and the 2022 Hudson Prize from Black Lawrence Press. Her stories have appeared in *West Branch, Pembroke Magazine, Willow Springs, Shenandoah, Copper Nickel, Blackbird, Fugue, Surreal South, The Chattahoochee Review, The Portland Review, Raleigh Review,* and elsewhere. Additionally, her story, "Percipient," won the *Willow Springs* Fiction Prize. Find her at www.katherineconner.info.

DOUG CRANDELL is the author of the Barnes & Noble Discover pick, *The Flawless Skin of Ugly People,* as well as three other novels and two memoirs. Doug's essays appear in the Pushcart Prize 2017 and 2022, and a short story in The *Best American Mystery Stories 2020.* He's a regular contributor to *The Sun.*

FINOLA DAVIDSON lives and writes in Durham, North Carolina.

JON DAVIS is the author of *Above the Bejeweled City, Fearless Now* and *Nameless* (Grid Books). He has received a Lannan Literary Award, the Lavan Prize, and two NEA Fellowships. Poems appeared recently in *Taos Journal of Poetry, Plume, Tampa Review, A House Called Tomorrow* (Copper Canyon), and *The Last Milkweed* (Tupelo Press).

PAUL FREIDINGER is a poet residing in Edisto Beach, South Carolina, where the ocean continues to rise. It keeps him awake at night. He has poems recently published or forthcoming in *Asheville Poetry Review, Folio, Florida Review, Grist, Innisfree Poetry Journal, Isthmus, North Dakota Quarterly, Portland Review, Roanoke Review, Santa Fe Literary Review, Southern Quarterly Review, Triggerfish Critical Review,* and *William & Mary Review.*

MARK HARRIS is a writer, editor, and book designer. His poems have appeared or are forthcoming in *The Hopkins Review, Noon, Ocean State Review, Shearsman, The Elephants,* and elsewhere. He works at Ornithopter Press.

NATALIE HOMER is the author of *Under the Broom Tree* (Autumn House Press). Her recent poetry has been published in *The Journal, Cream City Review, Potomac Review, Josephine Quarterly,* and others. She received an MFA from West Virginia University and lives in southwestern Pennsylvania.

KRISTA JAHNKE is a writer and strategic communications pro. Her fiction has appeared in *X-R-A-Y Literary Magazine, The Northwest Review, Peatsmoke Journal,* and elsewhere. She works for a nonprofit and lives with her husband, two teenage sons, and their very old cat outside of Detroit. Visit kristajahnkewriter.com to connect.

MATTHEW MINICUCCI is an award-winning author of four collections of poetry. His most recent, *Dual,* was just released this past fall by Acre Books. He is currently an Assistant Professor in the Blount Scholars Program at the University of Alabama.

SAM MOE is the author of two poetry books, with two more forthcoming in 2024: *Animal Heart* (3-Day Chapbook Contest) and *Cicatrizing the Daughters* (FlowerSong Press). She has received fellowships from the Longleaf Writer's Conference and Key West Literary Seminar, as well as writing residencies from VCCA and Château d'Orquevaux.

CYN NOONEY'S work has appeared in *New Ohio Review, The Penn Review, CRAFT, Chestnut Review, Ursa Minor, New York Times,* and elsewhere. In 2022, she was the winner of *ScreenCraft's* Cinematic Short Story Competition. She received her MFA from Pacific University and lives in the San Francisco Bay Area.

NICK RATTNER is a poet and story writer. Recent work has appeared in *Fence, Colorado Review, Pleiades,* and *Sixth Finch.* His translation of Juan Andrés García Román's *The Adoration* (2023) was recently published by Quantum Prose. He lives in Troy, New York, the city of crows.

AMY RATTO PARKS is the author of three collections of poetry and a verse novel, *Radial Bloom,* which Kirkus Review called "contemplative and original" and "brilliant, at once dense and ethereal." She lives and works in Missoula, Montana.

ANNA SCHACHNER is the author of the novel *You and I and Someone Else,* and her short fiction and nonfiction have appeared in many publications, including *Puerto del Sol, Hayden's Ferry Review,* and *The Sun.* She lives in Atlanta, where she is a freelance writer/editor/book coach.

PHILIP SCHAEFER'S collection *Bad Summon* (University of Utah Press, 2017) won the Agha Shahid Ali Poetry Prize, while individual poems have won contests published by *The Puritan, Meridian,* and *Passages North.* His work has been featured on Poem-A-Day, Poetry Daily, Verse Daily, and in The Poetry Society of America. He runs a modern Mexican restaurant called The Camino in Missoula, Montana.

ASHLEY SEITZ KRAMER has won the Ruth Stone Prize, the Schiff Prize, and the Utah Writers' Contest. Her book, *Museum of Distance* (2015), won the Zone 3 Press First Book Award. She holds an MFA in poetry from Vermont College and a PhD in education from the University of Utah.

MOLLIE SWAYNE is a writer and journalist living in Cedar Rapids, Iowa. Her work has appeared in *New American Writing, The Carolina Quarterly, Hobart,* and other publications. She was a prize-winning finalist for the 2023 Granum Foundation Prize, and she received her MFA from the University of Tennessee. She works in local news.

CECY VILLARRUEL is a first-generation American. She is a fan of cats, sunflowers, and living wages. She is an assistant professor in the English Department at Indiana University Northwest.

STEVEN WINN is a San Francisco writer and critic for Musical America, Opera, and the San Francisco Chronicle. His poetry has appeared in *32 Poems, The Able Muse, Antioch Review, Cimarron Review, Nimrod International, Poetry Daily, Prairie Schooner, Smartish Pace, Southern Poetry Review, Verse Daily,* and others.

STELLA WONG is the author of *Stem,* forthcoming from Princeton University Press, *Spooks,* winner of the Saturnalia Books Editors Prize, and *American Zero,* selected for the Two Sylvias Press Chapbook Prize by Danez Smith. A graduate of Harvard, the Iowa Writers' Workshop, and Columbia, Wong's poems have appeared in *Poetry, Colorado Review, Lana Turner, Bennington Review, American Poetry Review, Prairie Schooner,* and more.

www.ingramcontent.com/pod-product-compliance
Lightning Source LLC
Chambersburg PA
CBHW041754010726
47507CB00009B/387